The Duel

Ruskin Bond is known for his signature simplistic and witty writing style. He is the author of several bestselling short stories, novellas, collections, essays and children's books; and has contributed a number of poems and articles to various magazines and anthologies. At the age of twenty-three, he won the prestigious John Llewellyn Rhys Prize for his first novel, *The Room on the Roof*. He was also the recipient of the Padma Shri in 1999, Lifetime Achievement Award by the Delhi Government in 2012, and the Padma Bhushan in 2014.

Born in 1934, Ruskin Bond grew up in Jamnagar, Shimla, New Delhi and Dehradun. Apart from three years in the UK, he has spent all his life in India, and now lives in Landour, Mussoorie, with his adopted family.

The Duel

Selected and Compiled by
RUSKIN BOND

Published by
Rupa Publications India Pvt. Ltd 2019
7/16, Ansari Road, Daryaganj
New Delhi 110002

Sales centres:
Allahabad Bengaluru Chennai
Hyderabad Jaipur Kathmandu
Kolkata Mumbai

Copyright © Ruskin Bond 2019

This is a work of fiction. Names, characters, places and incidents are either the product of the author's imagination or are used fictitiously and any resemblance to any actual person, living or dead, events or locales is entirely coincidental.

All rights reserved.
No part of this publication may be reproduced, transmitted, or stored in a retrieval system, in any form or by any means, electronic, mechanical, photocopying, recording or otherwise, without the prior permission of the publisher.

ISBN: 978-93-5333-275-4

First impression 2019

10 9 8 7 6 5 4 3 2 1

Printed at HT Media Ltd, Gr. Noida

This book is sold subject to the condition that it shall not, by way of trade or otherwise, be lent, resold, hired out, or otherwise circulated, without the publisher's prior consent, in any form of binding or cover other than that in which it is published.

CONTENTS

Introduction	vii
The Duel *Wilkie Collins*	1
The Red-headed League *Arthur Conan Doyle*	18
The Cask of Amontillado *Edgar Allan Poe*	49
The Lodger *Marie Belloc Lowndes*	57
The Perfect Murder *Stacy Aumonier*	94
The Squaw *Bram Stoker*	114
Mrs Raeburn's Waxwork *Lady Eleanor Smith*	129
The Return of Imray *Rudyard Kipling*	144
The Empty House *Algernon Blackwood*	158

Chunia, Ayah   178
    Alice Perrin

Thurnley Abbey   186
    Perceval Landon

Gone Fishing   205
    Ruskin Bond

INTRODUCTION

In the little time that I had spent in my mother and stepfather's house in Dehra, I had made memories that I remember to this day; and not necessarily fond ones. They had a big enough house a little away from the centre of the town. That house had a dungeon-like room in its basement. With its wooden flooring and stone walls, that room felt every bit haunted.

Haunted as that room felt, I was always quite at peace in it. Never felt much of a punishment down there. Being locked in there gave me a chance to be alone and make up stories in my head from a very young age. I would imagine all sorts of creatures and phantoms coming into that dungeon and all kinds of duels taking place. It was a treat for all my horror fantasies. The supernatural has been a favourite genre since as far back as I can remember. I feel fear is the one emotion a person cannot hide. But in reading a scary story, we experience a 'safe fear'. At the back of our minds, we know that it isn't really happening. Or at least we hope it isn't!

Collected in this book are some of the most bone-chilling stories I have ever come across. From Wilkie Collins and Bram Stoker to Marie Belloc Lowndes, Lady Eleanor Smith, Rudyard Kipling, Arthur Conan Doyle, Alice Perrin and Algernon

Blackwood, among others—these are the tales of true horror that will surface best in the darkness and will send a chill down your spine when the night falls!

Ruskin Bond

THE DUEL

Wilkie Collins

The doctors could do no more for the dowager Lady Berrick. When the medical advisers of a lady who has reached seventy years of age recommend the mild climate of the South of France, they mean in plain language that they have arrived at the end of their resources. Her ladyship gave the mild climate a fair trial, and then decided (as she herself expressed it) to 'die at home'. Travelling slowly, she had reached Paris at the date when I last heard of her. It was then the beginning of November. A week later, I met with her nephew, Lewis Romayne, at the club.

'What brings you to London at this time of the year?' I asked.

'The fatality that pursues me,' he answered grimly. 'I am one of the unluckiest men living.'

He was thirty years old; he was not married; he was the enviable possessor of the tiny old country seat, called Vange Abbey; he had no poor relations; and he was one of the handsomest men in England. When I add that I am, myself, a retired army officer, with a wretched income, a disagreeable wife, four ugly children, and a burden of fifty years on my back, no one will be surprised to hear that I answered Romayne, with bitter sincerity, in these words:

'I wish to Heaven I could change places with you!'

'I wish to Heaven you could!' he burst out, with equal sincerity on his side. 'Read that.'

He handed me a letter addressed to him by the travelling medical attendant of Lady Berrick. After resting in Paris, the patient had continued her homeward journey as far as Boulogne. In her suffering condition, she was liable to sudden fits of caprice. An insurmountable horror of the Channel passage had got possession of her: she positively refused to be taken on board the steamboat. In this difficulty, the lady who held the post of her 'companion' had ventured on a suggestion. Would Lady Berrick consent to make the Channel passage if her nephew came to Boulogne expressly to accompany her on the voyage? The reply had been so immediately favourable, that the doctor lost no time in communicating with Mr Lewis Romayne. This was the substance of the letter.

It was needless to ask any more questions—Romayne was plainly on his way to Boulogne. I gave him some useful information. 'Try the oysters,' I said, 'at the restaurant on the pier.'

He never even thanked me. He was thinking entirely of himself.

'Just look at my position,' he said. 'I detest Boulogne; I cordially share my aunt's horror of the Channel passage; I had looked forward to some months of happy retirement in the country among my books—and what happens to me? I am brought to London in this season of fogs, to travel by the tidal train at seven tomorrow morning—and all for a woman with whom I have no sympathies in common. If I am not an unlucky man—who is?'

He spoke in a tone of vehement irritation which seemed to me, under the circumstances, to be simply absurd. But *my* nervous system is not the irritable system—sorely tried by night study and strong tea—of my friend Romayne. 'It's only a matter of two days,' I remarked, by way of reconciling him to his situation.

'How do I know that?' he retorted. 'In two days, the weather may be stormy. In two days, she may be too ill to be moved. Unfortunately, I am her heir; and I am told I must submit to any whim that seizes her. I'm rich enough already; I don't want her money. Besides, I dislike all travelling—and especially travelling alone. You are an idle man. If you were a good friend, you would offer to go with me.' He added, with the delicacy which was one of the redeeming points in his wayward character, 'Of course as my guest.'

I had known him long enough not to take offence at his reminding me, in this considerate way, that I was a poor man. The proposed change of scene tempted me. What did I care for the Channel passage? Besides, there was the irresistible attraction of getting away from home.

The end of it was that I accepted Romayne's invitation.

◆

Shortly after noon, on the next day, we were established at Boulogne—near Lady Berrick, but not at her hotel. 'If we live in the same house,' Romayne reminded me, 'we shall be bored by the companion and the doctor. Meetings on the stairs, you know, and exchanging bows and small talk.' He hated those trivial conventionalities of society, in which other people delight. When somebody once asked him in what company he felt most at ease, he made a shocking answer—he said, 'In the company of dogs.'

I waited for him on the pier while he went to see her ladyship. He joined me again with his bitterest smile. 'What did I tell you? She is not well enough to see me today. The doctor looks grave, and the companion puts her handkerchief to her eyes. We may be kept in this place for weeks to come.'

The afternoon proved to be rainy. Our early dinner was a bad one. This last circumstance tried his temper sorely. He was no gourmand; the question of cookery was (with him) purely a matter of digestion. Those late hours of study and that abuse of tea to which I have already alluded, had sadly injured his stomach. The doctors warned him of serious consequences to his nervous system, unless he altered his habits. He had little faith in medical science, and he greatly overrated the restorative capacity of his constitution. So far as I know, he had always neglected the doctors' advice.

The weather cleared towards evening, and we went out for a walk. We passed a church—a Roman Catholic church, of course—the doors of which were still open. Some poor women were kneeling at their prayers in the dim light. 'Wait a minute,' said Romayne. 'I am in a vile temper. Let me try to put myself into a better frame of mind.'

I followed him into the church. He knelt down in a dark corner by himself. I confess I was surprised. He had been baptized in the Church of England; but, so far as outward practice was concerned, he belonged to no religious community. I had often heard him speak with sincere reverence and admiration of the spirit of Christianity—but he never, to my knowledge, attended any place of public worship. When we met again outside the church, I asked if he had been converted to the Roman Catholic faith.

'No,' he said. 'I hate the inveterate striving of that priesthood after social influence and political power as cordially as the fiercest Protestant living. But let us not forget that the Church of Rome has great merits to set against great faults. Its system is administered with an admirable knowledge of the higher needs of human nature. Take as one example what you have just seen. The solemn tranquillity of that church, the poor people praying near me, the few words of prayer by which I silently united myself to my fellow creatures have calmed me, and done me good. In our country, I should have found the church closed, out-of-service hours.' He took my arm, and abruptly changed the subject. 'How will you occupy yourself,' he asked, 'if my aunt receives me tomorrow?'

I assured him that I should easily find ways and means of getting through the time. The next morning, a message came from Lady Berrick, to say that she would see her nephew after breakfast. Left by myself, I walked towards the pier, and met with a man who asked me to hire his boat. He had lines and bait, at my service. Most unfortunately, as the event proved, I decided on occupying an hour or two by sea fishing.

The wind shifted while we were out, and before we could get back to the harbour, the tide had turned against us. It was six o'clock when I arrived at the hotel. A little open carriage was waiting at the door. I found Romayne impatiently expecting me, and no signs of dinner on the table. He informed me that he had accepted an invitation, in which I was included, and promised to explain everything in the carriage.

Our driver took the road that led towards the High Town. I subordinated my curiosity to my sense of politeness, and asked for news of his aunt's health.

'She is seriously ill, poor soul,' he said. 'I am sorry I spoke so petulantly and so unfairly when we met at the club. The near prospect of death has developed qualities in her nature which I ought to have seen before this. No matter how it may be delayed, I will patiently wait her time for the crossing to England.'

So long as he believed himself to be in the right, he was, as to his actions and opinions, one of the most obstinate men I ever met with. But once let him be convinced that he was wrong, and he rushed into the other extreme—became needlessly distrustful of himself, and needlessly eager in seizing his opportunity of making atonement. In this latter mood, he was capable (with the best intentions) of committing acts of the most childish imprudence. With some misgivings, I asked how he had amused himself in my absence.

'I waited for you,' he said, 'till I lost all patience, and went out for a walk. First, I thought of going to the beach, but the smell of the harbour drove me back into the town; and there, oddly enough, I met with a man, a certain Captain Peterkin, who had been a friend of mine at college.'

'A visitor to Boulogne?' I inquired.

'Not exactly.'

'A resident?'

'Yes. The fact is, I lost sight of Peterkin when I left Oxford—and since that time, he seems to have drifted into difficulties. We had a long talk. He is living here, he tells me, until his affairs are settled.'

I needed no further enlightenment—Captain Peterkin stood as plainly revealed to me as if I had known him for years. 'Isn't it a little imprudent,' I said, 'to renew your acquaintance with a man of that sort? Couldn't you have passed him, with a bow?'

Romayne smiled uneasily. 'I dare say you're right,' he answered, 'But, remember, I had left my aunt, feeling ashamed of the unjust way in which I had thought and spoken of her. How did I know that I mightn't be wronging an old friend next, if I kept Peterkin at a distance? His present position may be as much his misfortune, poor fellow, as his fault. I was half inclined to pass him, as you say—but I distrusted my own judgement.

He held out his hand, and he was so glad to see me. It can't be helped now. I shall be anxious to hear your opinion of him.'

'Are we going to dine with Captain Peterkin?'

'Yes. I happened to mention that wretched dinner yesterday at our hotel. He said, "Come to my boarding-house. Out of Paris, there isn't such a table d'hote in France." I tried to get off it not caring, as you know, to go among strangers—I said I had a friend with me. He invited you most cordially to accompany me. More excuses on my part only led to a painful result. I hurt Peterkin's feelings. "I'm down in the world," he said, "and I'm not fit company for you and your friends. I beg your pardon for taking the liberty of inviting you!" He turned away with tears in his eyes. What could I do?'

I thought to myself, 'You could have lent him five pounds, and got rid of his invitation without the slightest difficulty.' If I had returned in reasonable time to go out with Romayne, we might not have met the captain—or, if we had met him, my presence would have prevented the confidential talk and the invitation that followed. I felt I was to blame—and yet, how could I help it? It was useless to remonstrate: the mischief was done.

We left the Old Town on our right hand, and drove on, past a little colony of suburban villas, to a house standing by itself, surrounded by a stone wall. As we crossed the front garden on our way to the door, I noticed against the side of the house two kennels, inhabited by two large watch-dogs. Was the proprietor afraid of thieves?

◆

The moment we were introduced to the drawing-room, my suspicions of the company we were likely to meet with were fully confirmed.

'Cards, billiards, and betting'—there was the inscription legibly written on the manner and appearance of Captain Peterkin. The bright-eyed yellow old lady who kept the boarding-house would have been worth five thousand pounds in jewellery alone, if the ornaments which profusely covered her had been genuine precious stones. The younger ladies present had their cheeks as highly rouged and their eyelids as elaborately pencilled in black as if they were going on the stage, instead of going to dinner. We found these fair creatures drinking Madeira as a whet to their appetites. Among the men, there were two who struck me as the most finished and complete blackguards whom I had ever met within all my experience, at home and abroad. One, with a brown face and a broken nose, was presented to us by the title of 'Commander', and was described as a person of great wealth and distinction in Peru, travelling for amusement. The other wore a military uniform and decorations, and was spoken of as 'the General.' A bold bullying manner, a fat sodden face, little leering eyes, and greasy-looking hands, made this man so repellent to me that I privately longed to kick him. Romayne had evidently been announced, before our arrival, as a landed gentleman with a large income. Men and women vied in servile attentions to him. When we went into the dining-room, the fascinating creature who sat next to him held her fan before her face, and so made a private interview of it between the rich Englishman and herself. With regard to the dinner, I shall only report that it justified Captain Peterkin's boast, in some degree at least. The wine was good, and the conversation became gay to the verge of indelicacy. Usually the most temperate of men, Romayne was tempted by his neighbours into drinking freely. I was unfortunately seated at the opposite extremity of the table, and I had no opportunity of warning him.

The dinner reached its conclusion, and we all returned

together, on the foreign plan, to coffee and cigars in the drawing-room. The women smoked, and drank liqueurs as well as coffee, with the men. One of them went to the piano, and a little impromptu ball followed, the ladies dancing with their cigarettes in their mouths. Keeping my eyes and ears on the alert, I saw an innocent-looking table, with a surface of rosewood, suddenly develop a substance of green cloth. At the same time, a neat little roulette-table made its appearance from a hiding-place in a sofa. Passing near the venerable landlady, I heard her ask the servant, in a whisper, 'if the dogs were loose?' After what I had observed, I could only conclude that the dogs were used as a patrol, to give the alarm in case of a descent of the police. It was plainly high time to thank Captain Peterkin for his hospitality, and to take our leave.

'We have had enough of this,' I whispered to Romayne in English. 'Let us go.'

In these days, it is a delusion to suppose that you can speak confidentially in the English language, when French people are within hearing. One of the ladies asked Romayne, tenderly, if he was tired of her already. Another reminded him that it was raining heavily (as we could all hear), and suggested waiting until it cleared up. The hideous General waved his greasy hand in the direction of the card table, and said, 'The game is waiting for us.'

Romayne was excited, but not stupefied, by the wine he had drunk. He answered, discreetly enough, 'I must beg you to excuse me; I am a poor card player.'

The General suddenly looked grave. 'You are speaking, sir, under a strange misapprehension,' he said. 'Our game is lansquenet—essentially a game of chance. With luck, the poorest player is a match for the whole table.'

Romayne persisted in his refusal. As a matter of course, I

supported him, with all needful care to avoid giving offence. The General took offence, nevertheless. He crossed his arms on his breast, and looked at us fiercely.

'Does this mean, gentlemen, that you distrust the company?' he asked.

The broken-nosed Commander, hearing the question, immediately joined us, in the interests of peace—bearing with him the elements of persuasion, under the form of a lady on his arm.

The lady stepped briskly forward, and tapped the General on the shoulder with her fan. 'I am one of the company,' she said, 'and I am sure Mr Romayne doesn't distrust *me*.' She turned to Romayne with her most irresistible smile. 'A gentleman always plays cards,' she resumed, 'when he has a lady for a partner. Let us join our interests at the table—and, dear Mr Romayne, don't risk too much!' She put her pretty little purse into his hand, and looked as if she had been in love with him for half her lifetime.

The fatal influence of the sex, assisted by wine, produced the inevitable result. Romayne allowed himself to be led to the card table. For a moment, the General delayed the beginning of the game. After what had happened, it was necessary that he should assert the strict sense of justice that was in him. 'We are all honourable men,' he began.

'And brave men,' the Commander added, admiring the General.

'And brave men,' the General admitted, admiring the Commander. 'Gentlemen, if I have been led into expressing myself with unnecessary warmth of feeling, I apologize, and regret it.'

'Nobly spoken!' the Commander pronounced. The General put his hand on his heart and bowed. The game began.

As the poorest man of the two, I had escaped the attentions lavished by the ladies on Romayne. At the same time, I was obliged to pay for my dinner, by taking some part in the proceedings of the evening. Small stakes were allowed, I found, at roulette; and, besides, the heavy chances in favour of the table made it hardly worth while to run the risk of cheating in this case. I placed myself next to the least rascally-looking man in the company, and played roulette.

For a wonder, I was successful at the first attempt. My neighbour handed me my winnings. 'I have lost every farthing I possess,' he whispered to me, piteously, 'and I have a wife and children at home.' I lent the poor wretch five francs. He smiled faintly as he looked at the money. 'It reminds me,' he said, 'of my last transaction, when I borrowed of that gentleman there, who is betting on the General's luck at the card table. Beware of employing him as I did. What do you think I got for my note of hand of four thousand francs? A hundred bottles of champagne, fifty bottles of ink, fifty bottles of blacking, three dozen handkerchiefs, two pictures by unknown masters, two shawls, one hundred maps, *and*—five francs.'

We went on playing. My luck deserted me; I lost, and lost, and lost again. From time to time, I looked round at the card table. The 'deal' had fallen early to the General, and it seemed to be indefinitely prolonged. A heap of notes and gold (won mainly from Romayne, as I afterwards discovered) lay before him. As for my neighbour, the unhappy possessor of the bottles of blacking, the pictures by unknown masters, and the rest of it, he won, and then rashly presumed on his good fortune. Deprived of his last farthing, he retired into a corner of the room, and consoled himself with a cigar. I had just risen, to follow his example, when a furious uproar burst out at the card table.

I saw Romayne spring up, and snatch the cards out of the

General's hand. 'You scoundrel!' he shouted, 'you are cheating!' The General started to his feet in a fury. 'You lie!' he cried. I attempted to interfere, but Romayne had already seen the necessity of controlling himself. 'A gentleman doesn't accept an insult from a swindler,' he said coolly. 'Accept this, then!' the General answered—and spat on him. In an instant, Romayne knocked him down.

The blow was dealt straight between his eyes: he was a gross big-boned man, and he fell heavily. For the time he was stunned. The women ran, screaming, out of the room. The peaceable Commander trembled from head to foot. Two of the men present, who, to give them their due, were no cowards, locked the doors. 'You don't go,' they said, 'till we see whether he recovers or not.' Cold water, assisted by the landlady's smelling salts, brought the General to his senses after a while. He whispered something to one of his friends, who immediately turned to me. 'The General challenges Mr Romayne,' he said. 'As one of his seconds, I demand an appointment for tomorrow morning.' I refused to make any appointment unless the doors were first unlocked, and we were left free to depart. 'Our carriage is waiting outside,' I added. 'If it returns to the hotel without us, there will be an inquiry.' This latter consideration had its effect. On their side, the doors were opened. On our side, the appointment was made. We left the house.

◆

We were punctual to the appointed hour—eight o'clock.

The second who acted with me was a French gentleman, a relative of one of the officers who had brought the challenge. At his suggestion, we had chosen the pistol as our weapon. Romayne, like most Englishmen at the present time, knew nothing of the use of the sword. He was almost equally inexperienced with the pistol.

Our opponents were late. They kept us waiting for more than ten minutes. It was not pleasant weather to wait in. The day had dawned damp and drizzling. A thick white fog was slowly rolling in on us from the sea.

When they did appear, the General was not among them. A tall, well-dressed young man saluted Romayne with stern courtesy, and said to a stranger who accompanied him, 'Explain the circumstances.'

The stranger proved to be a surgeon. He entered at once on the necessary explanation. The General was too ill to appear. He had been attacked that morning by a fit—the consequence of the blow that he had received. Under these circumstances, his eldest son (Maurice) was now on the ground to fight the duel, on his father's behalf; attended by the General's seconds, and with the General's full approval.

We instantly refused to allow the duel to take place, Romayne loudly declaring that he had no quarrel with the General's son. Upon this, Maurice broke away from his seconds; drew off one of his gloves; and stepping close up to Romayne, struck him on the face with the glove. 'Have you no quarrel with me now?' the young Frenchman asked. 'Must I spit on you, as my father did?' His seconds dragged him away, and apologized to us for the outbreak. But the mischief was done. Romayne's fiery temper flashed in his eyes. 'Load the pistols,' he said. After the insult publicly offered to him, and the outrage publicly threatened, there was no other course to take.

It had been left to us to produce the pistols. We therefore requested the seconds of our opponent to examine, and to load them. While this was being done, the advancing sea-fog so completely enveloped us, that the duelists were unable to see each other. We were obliged to wait for the chance of a partial clearing in the atmosphere. Romayne's temper had become calm again. The generosity of his nature spoke in the words which he now addressed to his seconds.

'After all,' he said, 'the young man is a good son—he is bent on redressing what he believes to be his father's wrong. Does his flipping his glove in my face matter to me? I think I shall fire in the air.'

'I shall refuse to act as your second if you do,' answered the French gentleman who was assisting us. 'The General's son is famous for his skill with the pistol. If you didn't see it in his face just now, I did—he means to kill you. Defend your life, sir!' I spoke quite as strongly, to the same purpose, when my turn came. Romayne yielded—he placed himself unreservedly in our hands.

In a quarter of an hour, the fog lifted a little. We measured the distance, having previously arranged (at my suggestion) that the two men should both fire at the same moment, at a given signal. Romayne's composure, as they faced each other, was, in a man of his irritable nervous temperament, really wonderful. I placed him sideways, in a position which in some degree lessened his danger, by lessening the surface exposed to the bullet. My French colleague put the pistol into his hand, and gave him the last word of advice. 'Let your arm hang loosely down, with the barrel of the pistol pointing straight to the ground. When you hear the signal, only lift your arm as far as the elbow; keep the elbow pressed against your side—and fire.' We could do no more for him. As we drew aside—I own it—my tongue was like a cinder in my mouth, and a horrid inner cold crept through me to the marrow of my bones.

The signal was given, and the two shots were fired at the same time.

My first look was at Romayne. He took off his hat, and handed it to me with a smile. His adversary's bullet had cut a piece out of the brim of his hat, on the right side. He had literally escaped by a hairbreadth.

While I was congratulating him, the fog gathered again more thickly than ever. Looking anxiously towards the ground occupied by our adversaries, we could only see vague, shadowy forms hurriedly crossing and re-crossing each other in the mist. Something had happened! My French colleague took my arm and pressed it significantly. 'Leave me to inquire,' he said. Romayne tried to follow; I held him back, neither of us exchanged a word.

The fog thickened and thickened, until nothing was to be seen. Once we heard the surgeon's voice, calling impatiently for a light to help him. No light appeared that we could see. Dreary as the fog itself, the silence gathered round us again. On a sudden it was broken, horribly broken, by another voice, strange to both of us, shrieking hysterically through the impenetrable mist. 'Where is he?' the voice cried, in the French language. 'Assassin! Assassin! Where are you?' Was it a woman? Or was it a boy? We heard nothing more. The effect upon Romayne was terrible to see. He who had calmly confronted the weapon lifted to kill him, shuddered dumbly like a terror-stricken animal. I put my arm round him, and hurried him away from the place.

We waited at the hotel until our French friend joined us. After a brief interval he appeared, announcing that the surgeon would follow him.

The duel had ended fatally. The chance course of the bullet, urged by Romayne's unpractised hand, had struck the General's son just above the right nostril—had penetrated to the back of his neck—and had communicated a fatal shock to the spinal marrow. He was a dead man before they could take him back to his father's house.

So far, our fears were confirmed. But there was something else to tell, for which our worst presentiments had not prepared us.

A younger brother of the fallen man (a boy of thirteen years old) had secretly followed the duelling party, on their way from his father's house—had hidden himself—and had seen the dreadful end. The seconds only knew of it when he burst out of his place of concealment, and fell on his knees by his dying brother's side. His were the frightful cries which we had heard from invisible lips. The slayer of his brother was the 'assassin' whom he had vainly tried to discover through the fathomless obscurity of the mist.

We both looked at Romayne. He silently looked back at us, like a man turned to stone. I tried to reason with him.

'Your life was at your opponent's mercy,' I said. 'It was *he* who was skilled in the use of the pistol; your risk was infinitely greater than his. Are you responsible for an accident? Rouse yourself, Romayne! Think of the time to come, when all this will be forgotten.'

'Never,' he said, 'to the end of my life.'

He made that reply in dull monotonous tones. His eyes looked wearily and vacantly straight before him. I spoke to him again. He remained impenetrably silent; he appeared not to hear, or not to understand me. The surgeon came in, while I was still at a loss what to say or do next. Without waiting to be asked for his opinion, he observed Romayne attentively, and then drew me away into the next room.

'Your friend is suffering from a severe nervous shock,' he said. 'Can you tell me anything of his habits of life?'

I mentioned the prolonged night studies, and the excessive use of tea. The surgeon shook his head.

'If you want my advice,' he proceeded, 'take him home at once. Don't subject him to further excitement, when the result of the duel is known in the town. If it ends in our appearing in a court of law, it will be a mere formality in this case, and you can surrender when the time comes. Leave me your address in London.'

I felt that the wisest thing I could do was to follow his advice. The boat crossed to Folkestone at an early hour that day—we had no time to lose. Romayne offered no objection to our return to England; he seemed perfectly careless of what became of him. 'Leave me quiet,' he said: 'and do as you like.' I wrote a few lines to Lady Berrick's medical attendant, informing him of the circumstances. A quarter of an hour afterwards, we were on board the steamboat.

THE RED-HEADED LEAGUE

Arthur Conan Doyle

I had called upon my friend, Mr Sherlock Holmes, one day in the autumn of last year, and found him in deep conversation with a very stout, florid-faced elderly gentleman, with fiery red hair. With an apology for my intrusion, I was about to withdraw, when Holmes pulled me abruptly into the room and closed the door behind me.

'You could not possibly have come at a better time, my dear Watson,' he said, cordially.

'I was afraid that you were engaged.'

'So I am. Very much so.'

'Then I can wait in the next room.'

'Not at all. This gentleman, Mr Wilson, has been my partner and helper in many of my most successful cases, and I have no doubt that he will be of the utmost use to me in yours also.'

The stout gentleman half rose from his chair and gave a bob of greeting, with a quick little questioning glance from his small, fat-encircled eyes.

'Try the settee,' said Holmes, relapsing into his armchair, and putting his finger tips together, as was his custom when in judicial moods. 'I know, my dear Watson, that you share my love of all that is bizarre and outside the conventions and humdrum routine of everyday life. You have shown your relish for it by the enthusiasm which has prompted you to chronicle, and, if you will excuse my saying so, somewhat to embellish so many of my own little adventures.'

'Your cases have indeed been of the greatest interest to me,' I observed.

'You will remember that I remarked the other day, just before we went into the very simple problem presented by Miss Mary Sutherland, that for strange effects and extraordinary combinations we must go to life itself, which is always far more daring than any effort of the imagination.'

'A proposition which I took the liberty of doubting.'

2

'You did, Doctor, but none the less you must come round to my view, for otherwise I shall keep on piling fact upon fact on you, until your reason breaks down under them and acknowledge me to be right. Now, Mr Jabez Wilson here has been good enough to call upon me this morning, and to begin a narrative which promises to be one of the most singular which I have listened to for some time. You have heard me remark that the strangest and most unique things are very often connected not with the larger but with the smaller crimes, and occasionally, indeed, where there is room for doubt whether any positive crime has been committed. As far as I have heard, it is impossible for me to say whether the present case is an instance of crime or not, but the course of events is certainly among the most singular that I have ever listened to. Perhaps, Mr Wilson, you would have the great kindness to recommence your narrative. I ask you, not merely because my friend, Dr Watson, has not heard the opening part, but also because the peculiar nature of the story makes me anxious to have every possible detail from your lips. As a rule, when I have heard some slight indication of the course of events, I am able to guide myself by the thousands of other similar cases which occur to my memory. In the present instance, I am forced to admit that the facts are, to the best of my belief, unique.'

The portly client puffed out his chest with an appearance of some little pride, and pulled a dirty and wrinkled newspaper from the inside pocket of his greatcoat. As he glanced down the advertisement column, with his head thrust forward, and the paper flattened out upon his knee, I took a good look at the man, and endeavoured, after the fashion of my companion, to read the indications which might be presented by his dress or appearance.

I did not gain very much, however, by my inspection. Our visitor bore every mark of being an average commonplace British tradesman—obese, pompous, and slow. He wore rather baggy grey shepherd's check trousers, a not over-clean black frock coat, unbuttoned in the front, and a drab waistcoat with a heavy brassy Albert chain, and a square pierced bit of metal dangling down as an ornament. A frayed top hat and a faded brown overcoat with a wrinkled velvet collar lay upon a chair beside him. Altogether, look as I would, there was nothing remarkable about the man save his blazing red head and the expression of extreme chagrin and discontent upon his features.

3

Sherlock Holmes's quick eye took in my occupation, and he shook his head with a smile as he noticed my questioning glances. 'Beyond the obvious facts that he has at some time done manual labour, that he takes snuff, that he is a Freemason, that he has been in China, and that he has done a considerable amount of writing lately, I can deduce nothing else.'

Mr Jabez Wilson started up in his chair, with his forefinger upon the paper, but his eyes upon my companion.

'How, in the name of good fortune, did you know all that, Mr Holmes?' he asked. 'How did you know, for example, that I did manual labour? It's as true as gospel, for I began as a ship's carpenter.'

'Your hands, my dear sir. Your right hand is quite a size larger than your left. You have worked with it and the muscles are more developed.'

'Well, the snuff, then, and the Freemasonry?'

'I won't insult your intelligence by telling you how I read that, especially as, rather against the strict rules of your order, you use an arc and compass breastpin.'

'Ah, of course, I forgot that. But the writing?'

'What else can be indicated by that right cuff so very shiny for five inches, and the left one with the smooth patch near the elbow where you rest it upon the desk.'

'Well, but China?'

'The fish which you have tattooed immediately above your wrist could only have been done in China. I have made a small study of tattoo marks, and have even contributed to the literature of the subject. That trick of staining the fishes' scales of a delicate pink is quite peculiar to China. When, in addition, I see a Chinese coin hanging from your watch chain, the matter becomes even more simple.'

4

Mr Jabez Wilson laughed heavily. 'Well, I never!' said he. 'I thought at first that you had done something clever, but I see that there was nothing in it after all.'

'I begin to think, Watson,' said Holmes, 'that I make a mistake in explaining. "Omne ignotom pro magnifico," you know, and my poor little reputation, such as it is, will suffer shipwreck if I am so candid. Can you not find the advertisement, Mr Wilson?'

'Yes, I have got it now,' he answered, with his thick, red finger planted halfway down the column. 'Here it is. This is what began it all. You just read it for yourself, sir.'

I took the paper from him and read as follows:

'TO THE RED-HEADED LEAGUE: On account of the bequest of the late Ezekiah Hopkins, of Lebanon, Pa., U.S.A., there is now another vacancy open which entitles a member of the League to a salary of four pounds a week for purely nominal services. All red-headed men who are sound in body and mind and above the age of twenty-one years are eligible. Apply in person on Monday, at eleven o'clock, to Duncan Ross, at the offices of the League, 7 Pope's Court, Fleet Street.'

'What on earth does this mean?' I ejaculated, after I had twice read over the extraordinary announcement.

Holmes chuckled and wriggled in his chair, as was his habit when in high spirits. 'It is a little off the beaten track, isn't it?' said he. 'And now, Mr Wilson, off you go at scratch, and tell us all about yourself, your household, and the effect which this advertisement had upon your fortunes. You will first make a note, Doctor, of the paper and the date.'

'It is *The Morning Chronicle* of 27 April 1890. Just two months ago.'

'Very good. Now, Mr Wilson.'

5

'Well, it is just as I have been telling you, Mr Sherlock Holmes,' said Jabez Wilson, mopping his forehead, 'I have a small pawnbroker's business at Saxe-Coburg Square, near the City. It's not a very large affair, and of late years, it has not done more than just give me a living. I used to be able to keep two assistants, but now I only keep one; and I would have a job to pay him but that he is willing to come for half wages, so as to learn the business.'

'What is the name of this obliging youth?' asked Sherlock Holmes.

'His name is Vincent Spaulding, and he's not such a youth either. It's hard to say his age. I should not wish a smarter assistant, Mr Holmes; and I know very well that he could better himself, and earn twice what I am able to give him. But, after all, if he is satisfied, why should I put ideas in his head?'

'Why, indeed? You seem most fortunate in having an employee who comes under the full market price. It is not a common experience among employers in this age. I didn't know that your assistant is not as remarkable as your advertisement.'

'Oh, he has his faults, too,' said Mr Wilson. 'Never was such a fellow for photography. Snapping away with a camera when he ought to be improving his mind, and then diving down into the cellar like a rabbit into its hole to develop his pictures. That is his main fault; but, on the whole, he's a good worker. There's no vice in him.'

'He is still with you, I presume?'

'Yes, sir. He and a girl of fourteen, who does a bit of simple cooking, and keeps the place clean—that's all I have in the house, for I am a widower, and never had any family. We live very quietly, sir, the three of us; and we keep a roof over our heads, and pay our debts, if we do nothing more.

6

'The first thing that put us out was that advertisement. Spaulding, he came down into the office just this day eight weeks, with this very paper in his hand, and he says:

"I wish to the Lord, Mr Wilson, that I was a red-headed man."

"Why that?" I asks.

"Why," says he, 'here's another vacancy on the League of the Red-headed Men. It's worth quite a little fortune to any man who gets it, and I understand that there are more vacancies than there are men, so that the trustees are at their wits' end what to do with the money. If my hair would only change colour here's a nice little crib all ready for me to step into."

"Why, what is it, then?" I asked. You see, Mr Holmes, I am a very stay-at-home man, and, as my business came to me instead of my having to go to it, I was often weeks on end without putting my foot over the doormat. In that way I didn't know much of what was going on outside, and I was always glad of a bit of news.'

"Have you never heard of the League of the Red-headed Men?" he asked, with his eyes open.

"Never."

"Why, I wonder at that, for you are eligible yourself for one of the vacancies."

"And what are they worth?" I asked.

"Oh, merely a couple of hundred a year, but the work is slight, and it need not interfere very much with one's other occupations."

'Well, you can easily think that that made me prick up my ears, for the business has not been very good for some years, and an extra couple of hundred would have been very handy.

"Tell me all about it," said I.

7

'"Well," said he, showing me the advertisement, "you can see for yourself that the League has a vacancy, and there is the address where you should apply for particulars. As far as I can make out, the League was founded by an American millionaire, Ezekiah Hopkins, who was very peculiar in his ways. He was himself red-headed, and he had a great sympathy for all red-headed men; so, when he died, it was found that he had left his enormous fortune in the hands of trustees, with instructions to apply the interest to the providing of easy berths to men whose hair is of that colour. From all I hear, it is splendid pay, and very little to do."

'"But," said I, "there would be millions of red-headed men who would apply."

'"Not so many as you might think," he answered. "You see it is really confined to Londoners, and to grown men. This American had started from London when he was young, and he wanted to do the old town a good turn. Then, again, I have heard it is of no use your applying if your hair is light red, or dark red, or anything but real, bright, blazing, fiery red. Now, if you cared to apply, Mr Wilson, you would just walk in; but perhaps it would hardly be worth your while to put yourself out of the way for the sake of a few hundred pounds."

'Now it is a fact, gentlemen, as you may see for yourselves, that my hair is of a very full and rich tint, so that it seemed to me that, if there was to be any competition in the matter, I stood as good a chance as any man that I had ever met. Vincent Spaulding seemed to know so much about it that I thought he might prove useful, so I just ordered him to put up the shutters for the day, and to come right away with me. He was very willing to have a holiday, so we shut the business up, and started off for the address that was given to us in the advertisement.'

8

'I never hope to see such a sight as that again, Mr Holmes. From north, south, east, and west every man who had a shade of red in his hair had tramped into the City to answer the advertisement. Fleet Street was choked with red-headed folk, and Pope's Court looked like a coster's orange barrow. I should not have thought there were so many in the whole country as were brought together by that single advertisement. Every shade of colour they were—straw, lemon, orange, brick, Irish setter, liver, clay; but, as Spaulding said, there were not many who had the real vivid flame-coloured tint. When I saw how many were waiting, I would have given it up in despair; but Spaulding would not hear of it. How he did it I could not imagine, but he pushed and pulled and butted until he got me through the crowd, and right up to the steps which led to the office. There was a double stream upon the stair, some going up in hope, and some coming back dejected; but we wedged in as well as we could, and soon found ourselves in the office.'

'Your experience has been a most entertaining one,' remarked Holmes, as his client paused and refreshed his memory with a huge pinch of snuff. 'Pray continue your very interesting statement.'

'There was nothing in the office but a couple of wooden chairs and a deal table, behind which sat a small man, with a head that was even redder than mine. He said a few words to each candidate as he came up, and then he always managed to find some fault in them which would disqualify them. Getting a vacancy did not seem to be such a very easy matter after all.

However, when our turn came, the little man was much more favourable to me than to any of the others, and he closed the door as we entered, so that he might have a private word with us.

'"This is Mr Jabez Wilson," said my assistant, "and he is willing to fill a vacancy in the League."

9

'"And he is admirably suited for it," the other answered. "He has every requirement. I cannot recall when I have seen anything so fine." He took a step backward, cocked his head on one side, and gazed at my hair until I felt quite bashful. Then suddenly he plunged forward, wrung my hand, and congratulated me warmly on my success.

'"It would be injustice to hesitate," said he. "You will, however, I am sure, excuse me for taking an obvious precaution." With that he seized my hair in both his hands, and tugged until I yelled with the pain. "There is water in your eyes," said he, as he released me. "I perceive that all is as it should be. But we have to be careful, for we have twice been deceived by wigs and once by paint. I could tell you tales of cobbler's wax which would disgust you with human nature." He stepped over to the window and shouted through it at the top of his voice that the vacancy was filled. A groan of disappointment came up from below, and the folk all trooped away in different directions, until there was not a red head to be seen except my own and that of the manager.

'"My name," said he, "is Mr Duncan Ross, and I am myself one of the pensioners upon the fund left by our noble benefactor. Are you a married man, Mr Wilson? Have you a family?"

'I answered that I had not.

'His face fell immediately.

"'Dear me!" he said, gravely, "that is very serious indeed! I am sorry to hear you say that. The fund was, of course, for the propagation and spread of the red heads as well as for their maintenance. It is exceedingly unfortunate that you should be a bachelor."

'My face lengthened at this, Mr Holmes, for I thought that I was not to have the vacancy after all; but, after thinking it over for a few minutes, he said that it would be all right.'

10

'"In the case of another," said he, "the objection might be fatal, but we must stretch a point in favour of a man with such a head of hair as yours. When shall you be able to enter upon your new duties?"

'"Well, it is a little awkward, for I have a business already," said I.

'"Oh, never mind about that, Mr Wilson!" said Vincent Spaulding. "I shall be able to look after that for you."

'"What would be the hours?" I asked.

'"Ten to two."

'Now a pawnbroker's business is mostly done of an evening, Mr Holmes, especially Thursday and Friday evenings, which is just before pay day; so it would suit me very well to earn a little in the mornings. Besides, I knew that my assistant was a good man, and that he would see to anything that turned up.

'"That would suit me very well," said I. "And the pay?"

'"Is four pounds a week."

'"And the work?"

'"Is purely nominal."

'"What do you call purely nominal?"

'"Well, you have to be in the office, or at least in the building, the whole time. If you leave, you forfeit your whole position forever. The will is very clear upon that point. You don't comply with the conditions if you budge from the office during that time."

"'It's only four hours a day, and I should not think of leaving,' said I.

"'No excuse will avail,' said Mr Duncan Ross, "neither sickness, nor business, nor anything else. There you must stay, or you lose your billet."

"'And the work?'

11

"'Is to copy out the *Encyclopaedia Britannica*. There is the first volume of it in that press. You must find your own ink, pens, and blotting paper, but we provide this table and chair. Will you be ready tomorrow?'

"'Certainly,' I answered.

"'Then, goodbye, Mr Jabez Wilson, and let me congratulate you once more on the important position which you have been fortunate enough to gain.' He bowed me out of the room, and I went home with my assistant, hardly knowing what to say or do, I was so pleased at my own good fortune.

'Well, I thought over the matter all day, and by evening I was in low spirits again; for I had quite persuaded myself that the whole affair must be some great hoax or fraud, though what its object might be I could not imagine. It seemed altogether past belief that anyone could make such a will, or that they would pay such a sum for doing anything so simple as copying out the *Encyclopaedia Britannica*. Vincent Spaulding did what he could to cheer me up, but by bed time, I had reasoned myself out of the whole thing. However, in the morning, I determined to have a look at it anyhow, so I bought a penny bottle of ink, and with a quill pen and seven sheets of foolscap paper, I started off for Pope's Court.

'Well, to my surprise and delight, everything was as right as possible. The table was set out ready for me, and Mr Duncan Ross was there to see that I got fairly to work. He started me off upon the letter A, and then he left me; but he would drop in from time to time to see that all was right with me. At two o'clock he bade me good-day, complimented me upon the amount that I had written, and locked the door of the office after me.

'This went on day after day, Mr Holmes, and on Saturday the manager came in and planked down four golden sovereigns for my week's work. It was the same next week, and the same the week after. Every morning I was there at ten, and every afternoon I left at two. By degrees Mr Duncan Ross took to coming in only once of a morning, and then, after a time, he did not come in at all. Still, of course, I never dared to leave the room for an instant, for I was not sure when he might come, and the billet was such a good one, and suited me so well, that I would not risk the loss of it.

12

'Eight weeks passed away like this, and I had written about Abbots, and Archery, and Armor, and Architecture, and Attica, and hoped with diligence that I might get on to the Bs before very long. It cost me something in foolscap, and I had pretty nearly filled a shelf with my writings. And then suddenly the whole business came to an end.'

'To an end?'

'Yes, sir. And no later than this morning. I went to my work as usual at ten o'clock, but the door was shut and locked, with a little square of cardboard hammered onto the middle of the panel with a tack. Here it is, and you can read for yourself.'

He held up a piece of white cardboard, about the size of a sheet of note paper. It read in this fashion:

'THE RED-HEADED LEAGUE IS DISSOLVED.
9 Oct. 1890.'

Sherlock Holmes and I surveyed this curt announcement and the rueful face behind it, until the comical side of the affair so completely overtopped every consideration that we both burst out into a roar of laughter.

'I cannot see that there is anything very funny,' cried our client, flushing up to the roots of his flaming head. 'If you can do nothing better than laugh at me, I can go elsewhere.'

'No, no,' cried Holmes, shoving him back into the chair from which he had half-risen. 'I really wouldn't miss your case for the world. It is most refreshingly unusual. But there is, if you will excuse my saying so, something just a little funny about it. Pray what steps did you take when you found the card upon the door?'

'I was staggered, sir. I did not know what to do. Then I called at the offices around, but none of them seemed to know anything about it. Finally, I went to the landlord, who is an accountant living on the ground floor, and I asked him if he could tell me what had become of the Red-headed League. He said that he had never heard of any such body. Then I asked him who Mr Duncan Ross was. He answered that the name was new to him.'

13

'"Well," said I, "the gentleman at No. 4."

'"What, the red-headed man?"

'"Yes."

'"Oh," said he, "his name was William Morris. He was a solicitor, and was using my room as a temporary convenience until his new premises were ready. He moved out yesterday."

'"Where could I find him?"

'"Oh, at his new offices. He did tell me the address. Yes, 17 King Edward Street, near St. Paul's."

'I started off, Mr Holmes, but when I got to that address it was a manufactory of artificial knee-caps, and no one in it had ever heard of either Mr William Morris or Mr Duncan Ross.'

'And what did you do then?' asked Holmes.

'I went home to Saxe-Coburg Square, and I took the advice of my assistant. But he could not help me in any way. He could only say that if I waited I should hear by post. But that was not quite good enough, Mr Holmes. I did not wish to lose such a place without a struggle, so, as I had heard that you were good enough to give advice to poor folk who were in need of it, I came right away to you.'

'And you did very wisely,' said Holmes. 'Your case is an exceedingly remarkable one, and I shall be happy to look into it. From what you have told me I think that it is possible that graver issues hang from it than might at first sight appear.'

'Grave enough!' said Mr Jabez Wilson. 'Why, I have lost four pound a week.'

'As far as you are personally concerned,' remarked Holmes, 'I do not see that you have any grievance against this extraordinary league. On the contrary, you are, as I understand, richer by some thirty pounds, to say nothing of the minute knowledge which you have gained on every subject which comes under the letter A. You have lost nothing by them.'

14

'No, sir. But I want to find out about them, and who they are, and what their object was in playing this prank—if it was a prank—upon me. It was a pretty expensive joke for them, for it cost them two-and-thirty pounds.'

'We shall endeavour to clear up these points for you. And, first, one or two questions, Mr Wilson. This assistant of yours who first called your attention to the advertisement—how long had he been with you?'

'About a month then.'

'How did he come?'

'In answer to an advertisement.'

'Was he the only applicant?'

'No, I had a dozen.'

'Why did you pick him?'

'Because he was handy and would come cheap.'

'At half wages, in fact.'

'Yes.'

'What is he like, this Vincent Spaulding?'

'Small, stout-built, very quick in his ways, no hair on his face, though he's not short of thirty. Has a white splash of acid upon his forehead.'

Holmes sat up in his chair in considerable excitement. 'I thought as much,' said he. 'Have you ever observed that his ears are pierced for earrings?'

'Yes, sir. He told me that a gypsy had done it for him when he was a lad.'

'Hum!' said Holmes, sinking back in deep thought. 'He is

still with you?'

'Oh, yes, sir; I have only just left him.'

'And has your business been attended to in your absence?'

15

'Nothing to complain of, sir. There's never very much to do of a morning.'

'That will do, Mr Wilson. I shall be happy to give you an opinion upon the subject in the course of a day or two. Today is Saturday, and I hope that by Monday we may come to a conclusion.'

'Well, Watson,' said Holmes, when our visitor had left us, 'what do you make of it all?'

'I make nothing of it,' I answered frankly. 'It is a most mysterious business.'

'As a rule,' said Holmes, 'the more bizarre a thing is, the less mysterious it proves to be. It is your commonplace, featureless crimes which are really puzzling, just as a commonplace face is the most difficult to identify. But I must be prompt over this matter.'

'What are you going to do, then?' I asked.

'To smoke,' he answered. 'It is quite a three-pipe problem, and I beg that you won't speak to me for fifty minutes.' He curled himself up in his chair, with his thin knees drawn up to his hawk-like nose, and there he sat with his eyes closed and his black clay pipe thrusting out like the bill of some strange bird. I had come to the conclusion that he had dropped asleep, and indeed was nodding myself, when he suddenly sprang out of his chair with the gesture of a man who has made up his mind, and put his pipe down upon the mantelpiece.

'Sarasate plays at St. James's Hall this afternoon,' he

remarked. 'What do you think, Watson? Could your patients spare you for a few hours?'

'I have nothing to do today. My practice is never very absorbing.'

'Then put on your hat and come. I am going through the City first, and we can have some lunch on the way. I observe that there is a good deal of German music on the programme, which is rather more to my taste than Italian or French. It is introspective, and I want to introspect. Come along!'

16

We travelled by the Underground as far as Aldersgate; and a short walk took us to Saxe-Coburg Square, the scene of the singular story which we had listened to in the morning. It was a poky, little, shabby-genteel place, where four lines of dingy, two-storied brick houses looked out into a small railed-in inclosure, where a lawn of weedy grass, and a few clumps of faded laurel bushes made a hard fight against a smoke-laden and uncongenial atmosphere. Three gilt balls and a brown board with JABEZ WILSON in white letters, upon a corner house, announced the place where our red-headed client carried on his business. Sherlock Holmes stopped in front of it with his head on one side, and looked it all over, with his eyes shining brightly between puckered lids. Then he walked slowly up the street, and then down again to the corner, still looking keenly at the houses. Finally he returned to the pawnbroker's and, having thumped vigorously upon the pavement with his stick two or three times, he went up to the door and knocked. It was instantly opened by a bright-looking, clean-shaven young fellow, who asked him to step in.

'Thank you,' said Holmes, 'I only wished to ask you how

you would go from here to the Strand.'

'Third right, fourth left,' answered the assistant, promptly, closing the door.

'Smart fellow, that,' observed Holmes as we walked away. 'He is, in my judgment, the fourth smartest man in London, and for daring I am not sure that he has not a claim to be third. I have known something of him before.'

'Evidently,' said I, 'Mr Wilson's assistant counts for a good deal in this mystery of the Red-headed League. I am sure that you inquired your way merely in order that you might see him.'

'Not him.'

'What then?'

'The knees of his trousers.'

17

'And what did you see?'

'What I expected to see.'

'Why did you beat the pavement?'

'My dear Doctor, this is a time for observation, not for talk. We are spies in an enemy's country. We know something of Saxe-Coburg Square. Let us now explore the parts which lie behind it.'

The road in which we found ourselves as we turned round the corner from the retired Saxe-Coburg Square presented as great a contrast to it as the front of a picture does to the back. It was one of the main arteries which convey the traffic of the City to the north and west. The roadway was blocked with the immense stream of commerce flowing in a double tide inward and outward, while the footpaths were black with the hurrying swarm of pedestrians. It was difficult to realize, as we looked at the line of fine shops and stately business premises, that they really abutted on the other side upon the faded and stagnant square which we had just quitted.

'Let me see,' said Holmes, standing at the corner, and glancing along the line, 'I should like just to remember the order of the houses here. It is a hobby of mine to have an exact knowledge of London. There is Mortimer's, the tobacconist; the little newspaper shop, the Coburg branch of the City and Suburban Bank, the Vegetarian Restaurant, and McFarlane's carriage-building depot. That carries us right on to the other block. And now, Doctor, we've done our work, so it's time we had some play. A sandwich and a cup of coffee, and then off to violin-land, where all is sweetness, and delicacy, and harmony, and there are no red-headed clients to vex us with their conundrums.'

My friend was an enthusiastic musician, being himself not only a very capable performer, but a composer of no ordinary merit. All the afternoon he sat in the stalls wrapped in the most perfect happiness, gently waving his long thin fingers in time to the music, while his gently smiling face and his languid, dreamy eyes were as unlike those of Holmes the sleuth-hound, Holmes the relentless, keen-witted, ready-handed criminal agent, as it was possible to conceive. In his singular character the dual nature alternately asserted itself, and his extreme exactness and astuteness represented, as I have often thought, the reaction against the poetic and contemplative mood which occasionally predominated in him. The swing of his nature took him from extreme languor to devouring energy; and, as I knew well, he was never so truly formidable as when, for days on end, he had been lounging in his armchair amid his improvisations and his black-letter editions. Then it was that the lust of the chase would suddenly come upon him, and that his brilliant reasoning power would rise to the level of intuition, until those who were unacquainted with his methods would look askance at him as on a man whose knowledge was not that of other mortals. When I saw him that afternoon so enwrapped in the music at St. James's Hall, I felt that an evil time might be coming upon those whom he had set himself to hunt down.

18

'You want to go home, no doubt, Doctor,' he remarked, as we emerged.

'Yes, it would be as well.'

'And I have some business to do which will take some hours. This business at Saxe-Coburg Square is serious.'

'Why serious?'

'A considerable crime is in contemplation. I have every reason to believe that we shall be in time to stop it. But today being Saturday rather complicates matters. I shall want your help tonight.'

'At what time?'

'Ten will be early enough.'

'I shall be at Baker Street at ten.'

'Very well. And, I say, Doctor! There may be some little danger, so kindly put your army revolver in your pocket.' He waved his hand, turned on his heel, and disappeared in an instant among the crowd.

I trust that I am not more dense than my neighbours, but I was always oppressed with a sense of my own stupidity in my dealings with Sherlock Holmes. Here I had heard what he had heard, I had seen what he had seen, and yet from his words it was evident that he saw clearly not only what had happened, but what was about to happen, while to me the whole business was still confused and grotesque. As I drove home to my house in Kensington I thought over it all, from the extraordinary story of the red-headed copier of the Encyclopaedia down to the visit to Saxe-Coburg Square, and the ominous words with which he had parted from me. What was this nocturnal expedition, and why should I go armed? Where were we going, and what were we to do? I had the hint from Holmes that this smooth-faced pawnbroker's assistant was a formidable man—a man who might play a deep game. I tried to puzzle it out, but gave it up in despair, and set the matter aside until night should bring an explanation.

19

It was a quarter past nine when I started from home and made my way across the Park, and so through Oxford Street to Baker Street. Two hansoms were standing at the door, and, as I entered the passage, I heard the sound of voices from above. On entering his room, I found Holmes in animated conversation with two men, one of whom I recognized as Peter Jones, the official police agent; while the other was a long, thin, sad-faced man, with a very shiny hat and oppressively respectable frock coat.

'Ha! Our party is complete,' said Holmes, buttoning up his pea-jacket, and taking his heavy hunting crop from the rack. 'Watson, I think you know Mr Jones, of Scotland Yard? Let me introduce you to Mr Merryweather, who is to be our companion in tonight's adventure.'

'We're hunting in couples again, Doctor, you see,' said Jones, in his consequential way. 'Our friend here is a wonderful man for starting a chase. All he wants is an old dog to help him do the running down.'

'I hope a wild goose may not prove to be the end of our chase,' observed Mr Merryweather gloomily.

'You may place considerable confidence in Mr Holmes, sir,' said the police agent loftily. 'He has his own little methods, which are, if he won't mind my saying so, just a little too theoretical and fantastic, but he has the makings of a detective in him. It is not too much to say that once or twice, as in that business of the Sholto murder and the Agra treasure, he has been more nearly correct than the official force.'

'Oh, if you say so, Mr Jones, it is all right!' said the stranger, with deference. 'Still, I confess that I miss my rubber. It is the first Saturday night for seven-and-twenty years that I have not had my rubber.'

'I think you will find,' said Sherlock Holmes, 'that you will play for a higher stake tonight than you have ever done yet, and that the play will be more exciting. For you, Mr Merryweather, the stake will be some thirty thousand pounds; and for you, Jones, it will be the man upon whom you wish to lay your hands.'

20

'John Clay, the murderer, thief, smasher, and forger. He's a young man, Mr Merryweather, but he is at the head of his profession, and I would rather have my bracelets on him than on any criminal in London. He's a remarkable man, this young John Clay. His grandfather was a Royal Duke, and he himself has been to Eton and Oxford. His brain is as cunning as his fingers, and though we meet signs of him at every turn, we never know where to find the man himself. He'll crack a crib in Scotland one week, and be raising money to build an orphanage in Cornwall the next. I've been on his track for years, and have never set eyes on him yet.'

'I hope that I may have the pleasure of introducing you tonight. I've had one or two little turns also with Mr John Clay, and I agree with you that he is at the head of his profession. It is past ten, however, and quite time that we started. If you two will take the first hansom, Watson and I will follow in the second.'

Sherlock Holmes was not very communicative during the long drive, and lay back in the cab humming the tunes which he had heard in the afternoon. We rattled through an endless labyrinth of gaslit streets until we emerged into Farringdon Street.

'We are close there now,' my friend remarked. 'This fellow Merryweather is a bank director and personally interested in the matter. I thought it as well to have Jones with us also. He is not a bad fellow, though an absolute imbecile in his profession. He has one positive virtue. He is as brave as a bulldog, and as tenacious as a lobster if he gets his claws upon anyone. Here we are, and they are waiting for us.'

We had reached the same crowded thoroughfare in which we had found ourselves in the morning. Our cabs were dismissed, and following the guidance of Mr Merryweather, we passed down a narrow passage, and through a side door which he opened for us. Within there was a small corridor, which ended in a very massive iron gate. This also was opened, and led down a flight of winding stone steps, which terminated at another formidable gate. Mr Merryweather stopped to light a lantern, and then conducted us down a dark, earth-smelling passage, and so, after opening a third door, into a huge vault or cellar, which was piled all round with crates and massive boxes.

21

'You are not very vulnerable from above,' Holmes remarked, as he held up the lantern and gazed about him.

'Nor from below,' said Mr Merryweather, striking his stick upon the flags which lined the floor. 'Why, dear me, it sounds quite hollow!' he remarked, looking up in surprise.

'I must really ask you to be a little more quiet,' said Holmes severely. 'You have already imperilled the whole success of our expedition. Might I beg that you would have the goodness to sit down upon one of those boxes, and not to interfere?'

The solemn Mr Merryweather perched himself upon a crate, with a very injured expression upon his face, while Holmes fell upon his knees upon the floor, and, with the lantern and a magnifying lens, began to examine minutely the cracks between the stones. A few seconds sufficed to satisfy him, for he sprang to his feet again, and put his glass in his pocket.

'We have at least an hour before us,' he remarked, 'for they can hardly take any steps until the good pawnbroker is safely in bed. Then they will not lose a minute, for the sooner they do their work the longer time they will have for their escape. We are at present, Doctor—as no doubt you have divined—in the cellar of the City branch of one of the principal London banks. Mr Merryweather is the chairman of directors, and he will explain to you that there are reasons why the more daring criminals of London should take a considerable interest in this cellar at present.'

'It is our French gold,' whispered the director. 'We have had several warnings that an attempt might be made upon it.'

'Your French gold?'

'Yes. We had occasion some months ago to strengthen our resources, and borrowed, for that purpose, thirty thousand napoleons from the Bank of France. It has become known that we have never had occasion to unpack the money, and that it is still lying in our cellar. The crate upon which I sit contains two thousand napoleons packed between layers of lead foil. Our reserve of bullion is much larger at present than is usually kept in a single branch office, and the directors have had misgivings upon the subject.'

22

'Which were very well justified,' observed Holmes. 'And now it is time that we arranged our little plans. I expect that within an hour matters will come to a head. In the meantime, Mr Merryweather, we must put the screen over that dark lantern.'

'And sit in the dark?'

'I am afraid so. I had brought a pack of cards in my pocket, and I thought that, as we were a *partie carrée*, you might have your rubber after all. But I see that the enemy's preparations have gone so far that we cannot risk the presence of a light. And, first of all, we must choose our positions. These are daring men, and, though we shall take them at a disadvantage, they may do us some harm, unless we are careful. I shall stand behind this crate, and do you conceal yourself behind those. Then, when I flash a light upon them, close in swiftly. If they fire, Watson, have no compunction about shooting them down.'

I placed my revolver, cocked, upon the top of the wooden case behind which I crouched. Holmes shot the slide across the front of his lantern, and left us in pitch darkness—such an absolute darkness as I have never before experienced. The smell of hot metal remained to assure us that the light was still there, ready to flash out at a moment's notice. To me, with my nerves worked up to a pitch of expectancy, there was something depressing and subduing in the sudden gloom, and in the cold, dank air of the vault.

'They have but one retreat,' whispered Holmes. 'That is back through the house into Saxe-Coburg Square. I hope that you have done what I asked you, Jones?'

'I have an inspector and two officers waiting at the front door.'

'Then we have stopped all the holes. And now we must be silent and wait.'

23

What a time it seemed! From comparing notes afterwards, it was but an hour and a quarter, yet it appeared to me that the night must have almost gone, and the dawn be breaking above us. My limbs were weary and stiff, for I feared to change my position, yet my nerves were worked up to the highest pitch of tension, and my hearing was so acute that I could not only hear the gentle breathing of my companions, but I could distinguish the deeper, heavier inbreath of the bulky Jones from the thin, sighing note of the bank director. From my position I could look over the case in the direction of the floor. Suddenly my eyes caught the glint of a light.

At first it was but a lurid spark upon the stone pavement. Then it lengthened out until it became a yellow line, and then, without any warning or sound, a gash seemed to open and a hand appeared, a white, almost womanly hand, which felt about in the centre of the little area of light. For a minute or more, the hand, with its writhing fingers, protruded out of the floor. Then it was withdrawn as suddenly as it appeared, and all was dark again save the single lurid spark, which marked a chink between the stones.

Its disappearance, however, was but momentary. With a rending, tearing sound, one of the broad white stones turned over upon its side, and left a square, gaping hole, through which streamed the light of a lantern. Over the edge there peeped a clean-cut, boyish face, which looked keenly about it, and then, with a hand on either side of the aperture, drew itself shoulder-high and waist-high, until one knee rested upon the edge. In another instant he stood at the side of the hole, and was hauling after him a companion, lithe and small like himself, with a pale face and a shock of very red hair.

'It's all clear,' he whispered. 'Have you the chisel and the bags? Great Scott! Jump, Archie, jump, and I'll swing for it!'

24

Sherlock Holmes had sprung out and seized the intruder by the collar. The other dived down the hole, and I heard the sound of rending cloth as Jones clutched at his skirts. The light flashed upon the barrel of a revolver, but Holmes's hunting crop came down on the man's wrist, and the pistol clinked upon the stone floor.

'It's no use, John Clay,' said Holmes blandly, 'you have no chance at all.'

'So I see,' the other answered, with the utmost coolness. 'I fancy that my pal is all right, though I see you have got his coat-tails.'

'There are three men waiting for him at the door,' said Holmes.

'Oh, indeed. You seem to have done the thing very completely. I must compliment you.'

'And I you,' Holmes answered. 'Your red-headed idea was very new and effective.'

'You'll see your pal again presently,' said Jones. 'He's quicker at climbing down holes than I am. Just hold out while I fix the derbies.'

'I beg that you will not touch me with your filthy hands,' remarked our prisoner, as the handcuffs clattered upon his wrists. 'You may not be aware that I have royal blood in my veins. Have the goodness also, when you address me, always to say "sir" and "please".'

'All right,' said Jones, with a stare and a snigger. 'Well, would you please, sir, march upstairs where we can get a cab to carry Your Highness to the police station?'

'That is better,' said John Clay serenely. He made a sweeping bow to the three of us, and walked quietly off in the custody of the detective.

'Really, Mr Holmes,' said Mr Merryweather, as we followed them from the cellar, 'I do not know how the bank can thank you or repay you. There is no doubt that you have detected and defeated in the most complete manner one of the most determined attempts at bank robbery that have ever come within my experience.'

25

'I have had one or two little scores of my own to settle with Mr John Clay,' said Holmes. 'I have been at some small expense over this matter, which I shall expect the bank to refund, but beyond that I am amply repaid by having had an experience which is in many ways unique, and by hearing the very remarkable narrative of the Red-headed League.'

'You see, Watson,' he explained, in the early hours of the morning, as we sat over a glass of whisky and soda in Baker Street, 'it was perfectly obvious from the first that the only possible object of this rather fantastic business of the advertisement of the League, and the copying of the Encyclopaedia must be to get this not over-bright pawnbroker out of the way for a number of hours every day. It was a curious way of managing it, but really it would be difficult to suggest a better. The method was no doubt suggested to Clay's ingenious mind by the colour of his accomplice's hair. The four pounds a week was a lure which must draw him, and what was it to them, who were playing for thousands? They put in the advertisement, one rogue has the temporary office, the other rogue incites the man to apply for it, and together they manage to secure his absence every morning in the week. From the time that I heard of the assistant having come for half wages, it was obvious to me that he had some strong motive for securing the situation.'

'But how could you guess what the motive was?'

'Had there been women in the house, I should have suspected a mere vulgar intrigue. That, however, was out of the question. The man's business was a small one, and there was nothing in his house which could account for such elaborate preparations, and such an expenditure as they were at. It must then be something out of the house. What could it be? I thought of the assistant's fondness for photography, and his trick of vanishing into the cellar. The cellar! There was the end of this tangled clue. Then I made inquiries as to this mysterious assistant, and found that I had to deal with one of the coolest and most daring criminals in London. He was doing something in the cellar—something which took many hours a day for months on end. What could it be, once more? I could think of nothing save that he was running a tunnel to some other building.'

26

'So far I had got when we went to visit the scene of action. I surprised you by beating upon the pavement with my stick. I was ascertaining whether the cellar stretched out in front or behind.

It was not in front. Then I rang the bell, and, as I hoped, the assistant answered it. We have had some skirmishes, but we had never set eyes upon each other before. I hardly looked at his face. His knees were what I wished to see. You must yourself have remarked how worn, wrinkled, and stained they were. They spoke of those hours of burrowing. The only remaining point was what they were burrowing for. I walked round the corner, saw that the City and Suburban Bank abutted on our friend's premises, and felt that I had solved my problem. When you drove home after the concert I called upon Scotland Yard, and upon the chairman of the bank directors, with the result that you have seen.'

'And how could you tell that they would make their attempt tonight?' I asked.

'Well, when they closed their League offices that was a sign that they cared no longer about Mr Jabez Wilson's presence; in other words, that they had completed their tunnel. But it was essential that they should use it soon, as it might be discovered, or the bullion might be removed. Saturday would suit them better than any other day, as it would give them two days for their escape. For all these reasons I expected them to come tonight.'

'You reasoned it out beautifully,' I exclaimed, in unfeigned admiration. 'It is so long a chain, and yet every link rings true.'

'It saved me from ennui,' he answered, yawning. 'Alas! I already feel it closing in upon me. My life is spent in one long effort to escape from the commonplaces of existence. These little problems help me to do so.'

'And you are a benefactor of the race,' said I. He shrugged his shoulders. 'Well, perhaps, after all, it is of some little use,' he remarked. '"L'homme c'est rien—l'oeuvre c'est tout," as Gustave Flaubert wrote to Georges Sands.'

THE CASK OF AMONTILLADO

Edgar Allan Poe

The thousand injuries of Fortunato I had borne as I best could, but when he ventured upon insult, I vowed revenge. You, who so well know the nature of my soul, will not suppose, however, that I gave utterance to a threat. *At length* I would be avenged; this was a point definitely settled—but the very definitiveness with which it was resolved, precluded the idea of risk. I must not only punish, but punish with impunity. A wrong is unredressed when retribution overtakes its redresser. It is equally unredressed when the avenger fails to make himself felt as such to him who has done the wrong.

It must be understood that neither by word nor deed had I given Fortunato cause to doubt my good will. I continued, as was my wont, to smile in his face, and he did not perceive that my smile *now* was at the thought of his immolation.

He had a weak point—this Fortunato—although in other regards he was a man to be respected and even feared. He prided himself on his connoisseurship in wine. Few Italians have the true virtuoso spirit. For the most part, their enthusiasm is adopted to suit the time and opportunity—to practise imposture upon the British and Austrian *millionaires*. In painting and gemmary, Fortunato, like his countrymen, was a quack—but in the matter of old wines he was sincere. In this respect I did not differ from him materially: I was skilful in the Italian vintages myself, and bought largely whenever I could.

It was about dusk, one evening during the supreme madness of the carnival season, that I encountered my friend. He accosted me with excessive warmth, for he had been drinking much. The man wore motley. He had on a tight-fitting parti-striped dress, and his head was surmounted by the conical cap and bells. I was so pleased to see him, that I thought I should never have done wringing his hand.

I said to him—'My dear Fortunato, you are luckily met. How remarkably well you are looking today! But I have received a pipe of what passes for Amontillado, and I have my doubts.'

'How?' said he. 'Amontillado? A pipe? Impossible! And in the middle of the carnival!'

'I have my doubts,' I replied; 'and I was silly enough to pay the full Amontillado price without consulting you in the matter. You were not to be found, and I was fearful of losing a bargain.'

'Amontillado!'

'I have my doubts.'

'Amontillado!'

'And I must satisfy them.'

'Amontillado!'

'As you are engaged, I am on my way to Luchesi. If any one has a critical turn, it is he. He will tell me—'

'Luchesi cannot tell Amontillado from Sherry.'

'And yet some fools will have it that his taste is a match for your own.'

'Come, let us go.'

'Whither?'

'To your vaults.'

'My friend, no; I will not impose upon your good nature. I perceive you have an engagement. Luchesi—'

'I have no engagement;—come.'

'My friend, no. It is not the engagement, but the severe cold with which I perceive you are afflicted. The vaults are insufferably damp. They are encrusted with nitre.'

'Let us go, nevertheless. The cold is merely nothing. Amontillado! You have been imposed upon. And as for Luchesi, he cannot distinguish Sherry from Amontillado.'

Thus speaking, Fortunato possessed himself of my arm. Putting on a mask of black silk, and drawing a *roquelaire* closely about my person, I suffered him to hurry me to my palazzo.

There were no attendants at home; they had absconded to make merry in honour of the time. I had told them that I should not return until the morning, and had given them explicit orders not to stir from the house. These orders were sufficient, I well knew, to insure their immediate disappearance, one and all, as soon as my back was turned.

I took from their sconces two flambeaux, and giving one to Fortunato, bowed him through several suites of rooms to the archway that led into the vaults. I passed down a long and winding staircase, requesting him to be cautious as he followed. We came at length to the foot of the descent, and stood together on the damp ground of the catacombs of the Montresors.

The gait of my friend was unsteady, and the bells upon his cap jingled as he strode.

'The pipe,' said he.

'It is farther on,' said I; 'but observe the white web-work which gleams from these cavern walls.'

He turned towards me, and looked into my eyes with two filmy orbs that distilled the rheum of intoxication.

'Nitre?' he asked, at length.

'Nitre,' I replied. 'How long have you had that cough?'

'Ugh! ugh! ugh!—ugh! ugh! ugh!—ugh! ugh! ugh!—ugh! ugh! ugh!—ugh! ugh! ugh!'

My poor friend found it impossible to reply for many minutes.

'It is nothing,' he said, at last.

'Come,' I said, with decision, 'we will go back; your health is precious. You are rich, respected, admired, beloved; you are happy, as once I was. You are a man to be missed. For me it is no matter. We will go back; you will be ill, and I cannot be responsible. Besides, there is Luchesi—'

'Enough,' he said; 'the cough is a mere nothing; it will not kill me. I shall not die of a cough.'

'True—true,' I replied; 'and, indeed, I had no intention of alarming you unnecessarily—but you should use all proper caution. A draught of this Medoc will defend us from the damps.'

Here I knocked off the neck of a bottle which I drew from a long row of its fellows that lay upon the mould.

'Drink,' I said, presenting him the wine.

He raised it to his lips with a leer. He paused and nodded to me familiarly, while his bells jingled.

'I drink,' he said, 'to the buried that repose around us.'

'And I to your long life.'

He again took my arm, and we proceeded.

'These vaults,' he said, 'are extensive.'

'The Montresors,' I replied, 'were a great and numerous family.'

'I forget your arms.'

'A huge human foot d'or, in a field azure; the foot crushes a serpent rampant whose fangs are imbedded in the heel.'

'And the motto?'

'Nemo me impune lacessit.'

'Good!' he said.

The wine sparkled in his eyes and the bells jingled. My own fancy grew warm with the Medoc. We had passed through walls of piled bones, with casks and puncheons intermingling, into the inmost recesses of catacombs. I paused again, and this time I made bold to seize Fortunato by an arm above the elbow.

'The nitre!' I said; 'see, it increases. It hangs like moss upon the vaults. We are below the river's bed. The drops of moisture trickle among the bones. Come, we will go back ere it is too late. Your cough—'

'It is nothing,' he said; 'let us go on. But first, another draught of the Medoc.'

I broke and reached him a flagon of De Grave. He emptied it at a breath. His eyes flashed with a fierce light. He laughed and threw the bottle upwards with a gesticulation I did not understand.

I looked at him in surprise. He repeated the movement—a grotesque one.

'You do not comprehend?' he said.

'Not I,' I replied.

'Then you are not of the brotherhood.'

'How?'

'You are not of the masons.'

'Yes, yes,' I said; 'yes, yes.'

'You? Impossible! A mason?'

'A mason,' I replied.

'A sign,' he said, 'a sign'.

'It is this,' I answered, producing a trowel from beneath the folds of my *roquelaire*.

'You jest,' he exclaimed, recoiling a few paces. 'But let us proceed to the Amontillado.'

'Be it so,' I said, replacing the tool beneath the cloak and again offering him my arm. He leaned upon it heavily. We continued our route in search of the Amontillado. We passed through a range of low arches, descended, passed on, and descending again, arrived at a deep crypt, in which the foulness of the air caused our flambeaux rather to glow than flame.

At the most remote end of the crypt there appeared another less spacious one. Its walls had been lined with human remains, piled to the vault overhead, in the fashion of the great catacombs of Paris. Three sides of this interior crypt were still ornamented in this manner. From the fourth side the bones had been thrown down, and lay promiscuously upon the earth, forming at one point a mound of some size. Within the wall thus exposed by the displacing of the bones, we perceived a still interior recess, in depth about four feet, in width three, in height six or seven. It seemed to have been constructed for no especial use within itself, but formed merely the interval between two of the colossal supports of the roof of the catacombs, and was backed by one of their circumscribing walls of solid granite.

It was in vain that Fortunato, uplifting his dull torch, endeavoured to pry into the depth of the recess. Its termination the feeble light did not enable us to see.

'Proceed,' I said; 'herein is the Amontillado. As for Luchesi—'

'He is an ignoramus,' interrupted my friend, as he stepped unsteadily forward, while I followed immediately at his heels. In an instant he had reached the extremity of the niche, and finding his progress arrested by the rock, stood stupidly bewildered. A moment more and I had fettered him to the granite. In its surface were two iron staples, distant from each other about two feet, horizontally. From one of these depended a short chain, from the other a padlock. Throwing the links about his waist, it was but the work of a few seconds to secure it. He was too much astounded to resist. Withdrawing the key I stepped back from the recess.

'Pass your hand,' I said, 'over the wall; you cannot help feeling the nitre. Indeed, it is *very* damp. Once more let me *implore* you to return. No? Then I must positively leave you. But I must first render you all the little attentions in my power.'

'The Amontillado!' ejaculated my friend, not yet recovered from his astonishment.

'True,' I replied; 'the Amontillado.'

As I said these words I busied myself among the pile of bones of which I have before spoken. Throwing them aside, I soon uncovered a quantity of building stone and mortar. With these materials and with the aid of my trowel, I began vigorously to wall up the entrance of the niche.

I had scarcely laid the first tier of the masonry when I discovered that the intoxication of Fortunato had in a great measure worn off. The earliest indication I had of this was a low moaning cry from the depth of the recess. It was *not* the cry of a drunken man. There was then a long and obstinate silence. I laid the second tier, and the third, and the fourth; and then I heard the furious vibrations of the chain. The noise lasted for several minutes, during which, that I might hearken to it with the more satisfaction, I ceased my labours and sat down upon the bones. When at last the clanking subsided, I resumed the trowel, and finished without interruption the fifth, the sixth, and the seventh tier. The wall was now nearly upon a level with my breast. I again paused, and holding the flambeaux over the mason-work, threw a few feeble rays upon the figure within.

A succession of loud and shrill screams, bursting suddenly from the throat of the chained form, seemed to thrust me violently back. For a brief moment I hesitated—I trembled. Unsheathing my rapier, I began to grope with it about the recess; but the thought of an instant reassured me. I placed my hand upon the solid fabric of the catacombs, and felt satisfied. I reapproached the wall; I replied to the yells of him who clamoured. I re-echoed—I aided—I surpassed them in volume and in strength. I did this, and the clamourer grew still.

It was now midnight, and my task was drawing to a close. I had completed the eighth, the ninth, and the tenth tier. I had finished a portion of the last and the eleventh; there remained but a single stone to be fitted and plastered in. I struggled with its weight; I placed it partially in its destined position. But now there came from out the niche a low laugh that erected the hair upon my head. It was succeeded by a sad voice, which I had difficulty in recognizing as that of the noble Fortunato. The voice said—

'Ha! ha! ha!—he! he! he!—a very good joke indeed—an excellent jest. We shall have many a rich laugh about it at the palazzo—he! he! he!—over our wine—he! he! he!'

'The Amontillado!' I said.

'He! he! he!—he! he! he!—yes, the Amontillado. But is it not getting late? Will not they be awaiting us at the palazzo, the Lady Fortunato and the rest? Let us be gone.'

'Yes,' I said, 'let us be gone.'

'For the love of God, Montresor!'

'Yes,' I said, 'for the love of God!'

But to these words I hearkened in vain for a reply. I grew impatient. I called aloud—

'Fortunato!'

No answer. I called again—

'Fortunato—'

No answer still. I thrust a torch through the remaining aperture and let it fall within. There came forth in reply only a jingling of the bells. My heart grew sick on account of the dampness of the catacombs. I hastened to make an end of my labour. I forced the last stone into its position; I plastered it up. Against the new masonry I re-erected the old rampart of bones. For the half of a century no mortal has disturbed them. *In pace requiescat!*

THE LODGER

Marie Belloc Lowndes

'There he is at last, and I'm glad of it, Ellen. 'Tain't a night you would wish a dog to be out in.'

Mr Bunting's voice was full of unmistakable relief. He was close to the fire, sitting back in a deep leather armchair—a clean-shaven, dapper man, still in outward appearance what he had been so long, and now no longer was—a self-respecting butler.

'You needn't feel so nervous about him; Mr Sleuth can look out for himself, all right.' Mrs Bunting spoke in a dry, rather tart tone. She was less emotional, better balanced, than was her husband. On her the marks of past servitude were less apparent, but they were there all the same—especially in her neat black stuff dress and scrupulously clean, plain collar and cuffs. Mrs Bunting, as a single woman, had been for long years what is known as a useful maid.

'I can't think why he wants to go out in such weather. He did it in last week's fog, too,' Bunting went on complaining.

'Well, it's none of your business—now, is it?'

'No; that's true enough. Still, 'twould be a very bad thing for us if anything happened to him. This lodger's the first bit of luck we've had for a very long time.'

Mrs Bunting made no answer to this remark. It was too obviously true to be worth answering. Also she was listening—following in imagination her lodger's quick, singularly quiet—'stealthy', she called it to herself—progress through the dark, fog-filled hall and up the staircase.

'It isn't safe for decent folk to be out in such weather—not unless they have something to do that won't wait till tomorrow.' Bunting had at last turned round. He was now looking straight into his wife's narrow, colourless face; he was an obstinate man, and liked to prove himself right. 'I read you out the accidents in Lloyd's yesterday—shocking, they were, and all brought about by the fog! And then, that 'orrid monster at his work again—'

'Monster?' repeated Mrs Bunting absently. She was trying to hear the lodger's footsteps overhead; but her husband went on as if there had been no interruption:

'It wouldn't be very pleasant to run up against such a party as that in the fog, eh?'

'What stuff you do talk!' she said sharply; and then she got up suddenly. Her husband's remark had disturbed her. She hated to think of such things as the terrible series of murders that were just then horrifying and exciting the nether world of London. Though she enjoyed pathos and sentiment—Mrs Bunting would listen with mild amusement to the details of a breach-of-promise action—she shrank from stories of either immorality or physical violence.

Mrs Bunting got up from the straight-backed chair on which she had been sitting. It would soon be time for supper.

She moved about the sitting-room, flecking off an imperceptible touch of dust here, straightening a piece of furniture there.

Bunting looked around once or twice. He would have liked to ask Ellen to leave off fidgeting, but he was mild and fond of peace, so he refrained. However, she soon gave over what irritated him, of her own accord.

But even then Mrs Bunting did not at once go down to the cold kitchen, where everything was in readiness for her simple cooking. Instead, she opened the door leading into the bedroom behind, and there, closing the door quietly, stepped back into the darkness and stood motionless, listening.

At first she heard nothing, but gradually there came the sound of someone moving about in the room just overhead; try as she might, however, it was impossible for her to guess what her lodger was doing. At last she heard him open the door leading out on the landing. That meant that he would spend the rest of the evening in the rather cheerless room above the drawing-room floor—oddly enough, he liked sitting there best, though the only warmth obtainable was from a gas-stove fed by a shilling-in-the-slot arrangement.

It was indeed true that Mr Sleuth had brought the Buntings luck, for at the time he had taken their rooms it had been touch-and-go with them.

After having each separately led the sheltered, impersonal, and, above all, the financially easy existence that is the compensation life offers to those men and women who deliberately take upon themselves the yoke of domestic service, these two, butler and useful maid, had suddenly, in middle age, determined to join their fortunes and savings.

Bunting was a widower; he had one pretty daughter, a girl of seventeen, who now lived, as had been the case ever since the death of her mother, with a prosperous aunt. His second wife had been reared in the Foundling Hospital, but she had gradually worked her way up into the higher ranks of the servant class and as useful maid she had saved quite a tidy sum of money.

Unluckily, misfortune had dogged Mr and Mrs Bunting from

the very first. The seaside place where they had begun by taking a lodging house became the scene of an epidemic. Then had followed a business experiment which had proved disastrous. But before going back into service, either together or separately, they had made up their minds to make one last effort, and, with the little money that remained to them, they had taken over the lease of a small house in the Marylebone Road.

Bunting, whose appearance was very good, had retained a connection with old employers and their friends, so he occasionally got a good job as waiter. During this last month, his jobs had perceptibly increased in number and in profit; Mrs Bunting was not superstitious, but it seemed that in this matter, as in everything else, Mr Sleuth, their new lodger, had brought them luck.

As she stood there, still listening intently in the darkness of the bedroom, she told herself, not for the first time, what Mr Sleuth's departure would mean to her and Bunting. It would almost certainly mean ruin.

Luckily, the lodger seemed entirely pleased both with the rooms and with his landlady. There was really no reason why he should ever leave such nice lodgings. Mrs Bunting shook off her vague sense of apprehension and unease. She turned round, took a step forward, and, feeling for the handle of the door giving into the passage, she opened it, and went down with light, firm steps into the kitchen.

She lit the gas and put a frying-pan on the stove, and then once more her mind reverted, as if in spite of herself, to her lodger, and there came back to Mrs Bunting, very vividly, the memory of all that had happened the day Mr Sleuth had taken her rooms.

The date of this excellent lodger's coming had been the twenty-ninth of December, and the time late afternoon. She and Bunting had been sitting, gloomily enough over their small banked-up fire. They had dined in the middle of the day—he on a couple of sausages, she on a little cold ham. They were utterly out of heart, each trying to pluck up courage to tell the other that it was no use trying any more. The two had also had a little tiff on that dreary afternoon. A newspaper-seller had come yelling down the Marylebone Road, shouting out, "Orrible murder in Whitechapel!' and just because Bunting had an old uncle living in the East End he had gone and bought a paper, and at a time, too, when every penny, nay, every half-penny, had its full value! Mrs Bunting remembered the circumstances because that murder in Whitechapel had been the first of these terrible cringes—there had been four since—which she would never allow Bunting to discuss in her presence, and yet which had of late begun to interest curiously, uncomfortably, ever her refined mind.

But, to return to the lodger. It was then, on that dreary afternoon, that suddenly there had come to the front door a tremulous, uncertain double knock.

Bunting ought to have got up, but he had gone on reading the paper and so Mrs Bunting, with the woman's greater courage, had gone out into the passage, turned up the gas, and opened the door to see who it could be. She remembered, as if it were yesterday instead of nigh on a month ago, Mr Sleuth's peculiar appearance. Tall, dark, lanky, an old-fashioned top hat concealing his high bald forehead, he had stood there, an odd figure of a man, blinking at her.

'I believe—is it not a fact that you let lodgings?' he had asked in a hesitating, whistling voice, a voice that she had known in a moment to be that of an educated man—of a gentleman. As he had stepped into the hall, she had noticed that in his right hand he held a narrow bag—a quite new bag of strong brown leather.

Everything had been settled in less than a quarter of an hour. Mr Sleuth had at once 'taken' to the drawing-room floor, and then, as Mrs Bunting eagerly lit the gas in the front room above, he had looked around him and said, rubbing his hands with a nervous movement, 'Capital—capital! This is just what I've been looking for!'

The sink had specially pleased him—the sink and the gas-stove. 'This is quite first-rate!' he had exclaimed, 'for I make all sorts of experiments. I am, you must understand, Mrs—er—Bunting, a man of science.' Then he had sat down—suddenly. 'I'm very tired,' he had said in a low tone, 'very tired indeed! I have been walking about all day.'

From the very first the lodger's manner had been odd, sometimes distant and abrupt, and then, for no reason at all that she could see, confidential and plaintively confiding. But Mrs Bunting was aware that eccentricity has always been a perquisite, as it were the special luxury of the well born and well educated. Scholars and such-like are never quite like other people.

And then, this particular gentleman had proved himself so eminently satisfactory as to the one thing that really matters to those who let lodgings. 'My name is Sleuth,' he said, 'S-l-e-u-t-h. Think of a hound, Mrs Bunting, and you'll never forget my name. I could give you references,' he had added, giving her, as she now remembered, a funny sidewise look, 'but I prefer to dispense with them. How much did you say? Twenty-three shillings a week, with attendance? Yes, that will suit me perfectly; and I'll begin by paying my first month's rent in advance. Now, four times twenty-three shillings is'—he looked at Mrs Bunting, and for the first time he smiled, a queer, wry smile—'ninety-two shillings.'

He had taken a handful of sovereigns out of his pocket and

put them down on the table. 'Look here,' he had said, 'there's five pounds; and you can keep the change, for I shall want you to do a little shopping for me tomorrow.'

After he had been in the house about an hour, the bell had rung, and the new lodger had asked Mrs Bunting if she could oblige him with the loan of a Bible. She brought up to him her best Bible, the one that had been given to her as a wedding present by a lady with whose mother she had lived for several years. This Bible and one other book, of which the odd name was *Cruden's Concordance*, formed Mr Sleuth's only reading: he spent hours each day poring over the Old Testament and over the volume which Mrs Bunting had at last decided to be a queer kind of index to the Book.

However, to return to the lodger's first arrival. He had had no luggage with him, barring the small brown bag, but very soon parcels had begun to arrive addressed to Mr Sleuth, and it was then that Mrs Bunting first became curious. These parcels were full of clothes; but it was quite clear to the landlady's feminine eye that none of these clothes had been made for Mr Sleuth. They were, in fact, second-hand clothes, bought at good second-hand places, each marked, when marked at all, with a different name. And the really extraordinary thing was that occasionally a complete suit disappeared—became, as it were, obliterated from the lodger's wardrobe.

As for the bag he had brought with him, Mrs Bunting had never caught sight of it again. And this also was certainly very strange.

Mrs Bunting thought a great deal about that bag. She often wondered what had been in it; not a nightshirt and comb and brush, as she had at first supposed, for Mr Sleuth had asked her to go out and buy him a brush and comb and toothbrush the morning after his arrival. That fact was specially impressed on her memory, for at the little shop, a barber's, where she had purchased the brush and comb, the foreigner who had served her had insisted on telling her some of the horrible details of the murder that had taken place the day before in Whitechapel, and it had upset her very much.

As to where the bag was now, it was probably locked up in the lower part of a chiffonnier in the front sitting-room. Mr Sleuth evidently always carried the key of the little cupboard on his person, for Mrs Bunting, though she looked well for it, had never been able to find it.

And yet, never was there a more confiding or trusting gentleman. The first four days that he had been with them he had allowed his money—the considerable sum of one hundred and eighty-four pounds in gold—to lie about wrapped up in pieces of paper on his dressing-table. This was a very foolish, indeed a wrong thing to do, as she had allowed herself respectfully to point out to him; but as an only answer he had laughed, a loud, discordant shout of laughter.

Mr Sleuth had many other odd ways; but Mrs Bunting, a true woman in spite of her prim manner and love of order, had an infinite patience with masculine vagaries.

On the first morning of Mr Sleuth's stay in the Buntings's house, while Mrs Bunting was out buying things for him, the new lodger had turned most of the pictures and photographs hanging in his sitting-room with their faces to the wall! But this queer action on Mr Sleuth's part had not surprised Mrs Bunting as much as it might have done; it recalled an incident of her long-past youth—something that had happened a matter of twenty years ago, at a time when Mrs Bunting, then the still youthful Ellen Cottrell, had been maid to an old lady. The old lady had a favourite nephew, a bright, jolly young gentleman who had been learning to paint animals in Paris; and it was he who had had the impudence, early one summer morning, to turn to the wall six beautiful engravings of paintings done by the famous Mr Landseer! The old lady thought the world of those pictures, but her nephew, as the only excuse for the extraordinary thing he had done, had observed that 'they put his eye out'.

Mr Sleuth's excuse had been much the same; for, when Mrs Bunting had come into his sitting-room and found all her pictures, or at any rate all those of her pictures that happened to be portraits of ladies, with their faces to the wall, he had offered an only explanation, 'Those women's eyes follow me about.' Mrs Bunting had gradually become aware that Mr Sleuth had a fear and dislike of women. When she was 'doing' the staircase and landing, she often heard him reading bits of the Bible aloud to himself, and in the majority of instances the texts he chose contained uncomplimentary reference to her own sex. Only today she had stopped and listened while he uttered threateningly the awful words, 'A strange woman is a narrow pit. She also lieth in wait as for a prey, and increaseth the transgressors among men.' There had been a pause, and then had come, in a high singsong, 'Her house is the way to hell, going down to the chambers of death.' It had made Mrs Bunting feel quite queer.

The lodger's daily habits were also peculiar. He stayed in bed all morning, and sometimes part of the afternoon, and he never went out before the street lamps were alight. Then, there was his dislike of an open fire; he generally sat in the top front room, and while there he always used the large gas-stove, not only for his experiments, which he carried on at night, but also in the daytime, for warmth.

But there! Where was the use of worrying about the lodger's funny ways? Of course, Mr Sleuth was eccentric; if he hadn't been 'just a leetle "touched" upstairs'—as Bunting had once described it—he wouldn't be their lodger now; he would be living in a quite different sort of way with some of his relations, or with a friend of his own class.

Mrs Bunting, while these thoughts galloped disconnectedly through her brain, went on with her cooking, doing everything with a certain delicate and clean precision.

While in the middle of making the toast on which was to be poured some melted cheese, she suddenly heard a noise, or rather a series of noises. Shuffling, hesitating steps were creaking down the house above. She looked up and listened. Surely Mr Sleuth was not going out again into the cold, foggy night? But no; for the sounds did not continue down the passage leading to the front door.

The heavy steps were coming slowly down the kitchen stairs. Nearer and nearer came the thudding sounds, and Mrs Bunting's heart began to beat as if in response. She put out the gas-stove, unheedful of the fact that the cheese would stiffen and spoil in the cold air; and then she turned and faced the door. There was a fumbling at the handle, and a moment later the door opened and revealed, as she had known it would, her lodger.

Mr Sleuth was clad in a plaid dressing-gown, and in his hand was a candle. When he saw the lit-up kitchen, and the woman standing in it, he looked inexplicably taken aback, almost aghast.

'Yes, sir? What can I do for you, sir? I hope you didn't ring, sir?' Mrs Bunting did not come forward to meet her lodger; instead, she held her ground in front of the stove. Mr Sleuth had no business to come down like this into her kitchen.

'No, I—I didn't ring,' he stammered; 'I didn't know you were down here, Mrs Bunting. Please excuse my costume. The truth is, my gas-stove has gone wrong, or, rather, that shilling in-the-slot arrangement has done so. I came down to see if *you* had a gas-stove. I am going to ask leave to use it tonight for an experiment I want to make.'

Mrs Bunting felt troubled—oddly, unnaturally troubled. Why couldn't the lodger's experiment wait till tomorrow? 'Oh, certainly, sir; but you will find it very cold down here.' She looked round her dubiously.

'It seems most pleasantly warm,' he observed, 'warm and cosy after my cold room upstairs.'

'Won't you let me make you a fire?' Mrs Bunting's housewifely instincts were roused. 'Do let me make you a fire in your bedroom, sir; I'm sure you ought to have one there these cold nights.'

'By no means—I mean, I would prefer not. I do not like an open fire, Mrs Bunting.' He frowned, and still stood, a strange-looking figure, just inside the kitchen door.

'Do you want to use this stove now, sir? Is there anything I can do to help you?'

'No, not now—thank you all the same, Mrs Bunting. I shall come down later, altogether later—probably after you and your husband have gone to bed. But I should be much obliged if you would see that the gas people come tomorrow and put my stove in order.'

'Perhaps Bunting could put it right for you, sir. I'll ask him to go up.'

'No, no—I don't want anything of that sort done tonight. Besides, he couldn't put it right. The cause of the trouble is quite simple. The machine is choked up with shillings: a foolish plan, so I have always felt it to be.'

Mr Sleuth spoke very pettishly, with far more heat than he was wont to speak; but Mrs Bunting sympathized with him. She had always suspected those slot-machines to be as dishonest as if they were human. It was dreadful, the way they swallowed up the shillings!

As if he were divining her thoughts, Mr Sleuth, walking

forward, stared up at the kitchen slot-machine. 'Is it nearly full?' he asked abruptly. 'I expect my experiment will take some time, Mrs Bunting.'

'Oh, no, sir; there's plenty of room for shillings there still. We don't use our stove as much as you do yours, sir. I'm never in the kitchen a minute longer than I can help in this cold weather.'

And then, with him preceding her, Mrs Bunting and her lodger made a slow progress to the ground floor. There Mr Sleuth courteously bade his landlady goodnight, and proceeded upstairs to his own apartment.

Mrs Bunting again went down into her kitchen, again she lit the stove, and again she cooked the toasted cheese. But she felt unnerved, afraid of she knew not what. The place seemed to her alive with alien presences, and once she caught herself listening, which was absurd, for of course she could not hope to hear what her lodger was doing two, if not three, flights upstairs. She had never been able to discover what Mr Sleuth's experiments really were; all she knew was that they required a very high degree of heat.

The Buntings went to bed early that night. But Mrs Bunting intended to stay awake. She wanted to know at what hour of the night her lodger would come down into the kitchen, and, above all, she was anxious as to how long he would stay there. But she had had a long day, and presently she fell asleep.

The church clock hard by struck two in the morning, and suddenly Mrs Bunting awoke. She felt sharply annoyed with herself. How could she have dropped off like that? Mr Sleuth must have been down and up again hours ago.

Then, gradually, she became aware of a faint acrid odour; elusive, almost intangible, it yet seemed to encompass her and the snoring man by her side almost as a vapour might have done.

Mrs Bunting sat up in bed and sniffed; and then, in spite

of the cold, she quietly crept out of the nice, warm bedclothes and crawled along to the bottom of the bed. There Mr Sleuth's landlady did a very curious thing; she leaned over the brass rail and put her face close to the hinge of the door. Yes, it was from there that this strange, horrible odour was coming; the smell must be very strong in the passage. Mrs Bunting thought she knew now what became of those suits of clothes of Mr Sleuth's that disappeared.

As she crept back, shivering, under the bedclothes, she longed to give her sleeping husband a good shake, and in fancy she heard herself saying: 'Bunting, get up! There is something strange going on downstairs that we ought to know about.'

But Mr Sleuth's landlady, as she lay by her husband's side, listening with painful intentness, knew very well that she would do nothing of the sort. The lodger had a right to destroy his clothes by burning if the fancy took him. What if he did make a certain amount of mess, a certain amount of smell, in her nice kitchen? Was he not—was he not such a good lodger! If they did anything to upset him, where could they ever hope to get another like him?

Three o'clock struck before Mrs Bunting heard slow, heavy steps creaking up her kitchen stairs. But Mr Sleuth did not go straight up to his own quarters, as she expected him to do. Instead, he went to the front door, and, opening it, put it on the chain. At the end of ten minutes or so he closed the front door, and by that time Mrs Bunting had divined why the lodger had behaved in this strange fashion—it must have been to get the strong acrid smell of burning wool out of the passage. But Mrs Bunting felt as if she herself would never get rid of the horrible odour. She felt herself to be all smell.

At last the unhappy woman fell into a deep, troubled sleep; and then she dreamed a most terrible and unnatural dream;

hoarse voices seemed to be shouting in her ear, "'Orrible murder off the Edgeware Road!' Then three words, indistinctly uttered, followed by '—at his work again! Awful details!'

Even in her dream Mrs Bunting felt angered and impatient; she knew so well why she was being disturbed by this horrid nightmare. It was because of Bunting—Bunting, who insisted on talking to her of those frightful murders, in which only morbid, vulgar-minded people took any interest. Why, even now, in her dream, she could hear her husband speaking to her about it.

'Ellen'—so she heard Bunting say in her ear—'Ellen, my dear, I am just going to get up to get a paper. It's after seven o'clock.'

Mrs Bunting sat up in bed. The shouting, nay, worse, the sound of tramping, hurrying feet smote on her ears. It had been no nightmare, then, but something infinitely worse—reality. Why couldn't Bunting have lain quietly in bed awhile longer, and let his poor wife go on dreaming? The most awful dream would have been easier to bear than this awakening.

She heard her husband go to the front door, and, as he bought the paper, exchange a few excited words with the newspaper boy. Then he came back and began silently moving about the room.

'Well!' she cried. 'Why don't you tell me about it?'

'I thought you'd rather not hear.'

'Of course I like to know what happens close to our own front door!' she snapped out.

And then he read out a piece of the newspaper—only a few lines, after all—telling in brief, unemotional language that the body of a woman, apparently done to death in a peculiarly atrocious fashion some hours before, had been found in a passage leading to a disused warehouse off the Marylebone Road.

'It serves that sort of hussy right!' was Mrs Bunting's only comment.

When Mrs Bunting went down into the kitchen, everything there looked just as she had left it, and there was no trace of the acrid smell she had expected to find there. Instead, the cavernous whitewashed room was full of fog, and she noticed that, though the shutters were bolted and barred as she had left them, the windows behind them had been widely opened to the air. She, of course, had left them shut.

She stooped and flung open the oven door of her gas-stove. Yes, it was as she had expected; a fierce heat had been generated there since she had last used the oven, and a mass of black, gluey soot had fallen through to the stone floor below.

Mrs Bunting took the ham and eggs that she had bought the previous day for her own and Bunting's breakfast, and broiled them over the gas-ring in their sitting-room. Her husband watched her in surprised silence. She had never done such a thing before.

'I couldn't stay down there,' she said, 'it was so cold and foggy. I thought I'd make breakfast up here, just for today.'

'Yes,' he said kindly; 'that's quite right, Ellen. I think you've done quite right, my dear.'

But, when it came to the point, his wife could not eat any of the nice breakfast she had got ready; she only had another cup of tea.

'Are you ill?' Bunting asked solicitously.

'No,' she said shortly; 'of course I'm not ill. Don't be silly! The thought of that horrible thing happening so close by has upset me. Just hark to them, now!'

Through their closed windows penetrated the sound of scurrying feet and loud, ribald laughter. A crowd, nay, a mob, hastened to and from the scene of the murder.

Mrs Bunting made her husband lock the front gate. 'I don't want any of those ghouls in here!' she exclaimed angrily. And then, 'What a lot of idle people there must be in the world,' she said.

The coming and going went on all day. Mrs Bunting stayed indoors; Bunting went out. After all, the ex-butler was human— it was natural that he should feel thrilled and excited. All their neighbours were the same. His wife wasn't reasonable about such things. She quarrelled with him when he didn't tell her anything, and yet he was sure she would have been angry with him if he had said very much about it.

The lodger's bell rang about two o'clock, and Mrs Bunting prepared the simple luncheon that was also his breakfast. As she rested the tray a minute on the drawing-room floor landing, she heard Mr Sleuth's high, quavering voice reading aloud the words:

'She saith to him, Stolen waters are sweet, and bread eaten in secret is pleasant. But he knoweth not that the dead are there; and that her guests are in the depths of hell.'

The landlady turned the handle of the door and walked in with the tray. Mr Sleuth was sitting close by the window, and Mrs Bunting's Bible lay open before him. As she came in, he hastily closed the Bible and looked down at the crowd walking along the Marylebone Road.

'There seem a great many people out today,' he observed, without looking round.

'Yes, sir, there do.' Mrs Bunting said nothing more, and offered no other explanation; and the lodger, as he at last turned to his landlady, smiled pleasantly. He had acquired a great liking and respect for this well-behaved, taciturn woman; she was the first person for whom he had felt any such feeling for many years past.

He took a half sovereign out of his waistcoat pocket; Mrs Bunting noticed that it was not the same waistcoat Mr Sleuth had been wearing the day before. 'Will you please accept this half sovereign for the use of your kitchen last night?' he said. 'I made as little mess as I could, but I was carrying on a rather elaborate experiment.'

She held out her hand, hesitated, and then took the coin. As she walked down the stairs, the winter sun, a yellow ball hanging in the smoky sky, glinted in on Mrs Bunting, and lent blood-red gleams, or so it seemed to her, to the piece of gold she was holding in her hand.

2

It was a very cold night—so cold, so windy, so snow-laden the atmosphere, that every one who could do so stayed indoors. Bunting, however, was on his way home from what had proved a very pleasant job; he had been acting as waiter at a young lady's birthday party, and a remarkable piece of luck had come his way. The young lady had come into a fortune that day, and she had had the gracious, the surprising thought of presenting each of the hired waiters with a sovereign.

This birthday treat had put him in mind of another birthday. His daughter Daisy would be eighteen the following Saturday. Why shouldn't he send her a postal order for half a sovereign, so that she might come up and spend her birthday in London?

Having Daisy for three or four days would cheer up Ellen. Mr Bunting, slackening his footsteps, began to think with puzzled concern of how queer his wife had seemed lately. She had become so nervous, so 'jumpy,' that he didn't know what to make of her sometimes. She had never been a really good-tempered woman—your capable, self-respecting woman seldom is—but she had never been like what she was now. Of late, she sometimes got quite hysterical; he had let fall a sharp word to her the other day, and she had sat down on a chair, thrown her black apron over her face, and burst out sobbing violently.

During the last ten days Ellen had taken to talking in her sleep. 'No, no, no!' she had cried out, only the night before. 'It isn't true! I won't have it said! It's a lie!' And there had been a wail of horrible fear and revolt in her unusually quiet, mincing voice. Yes, it would certainly be a good thing for her to have Daisy's company for a bit. Whew! It *was* cold; and Bunting had stupidly forgotten his gloves. He put his hands in his pockets to keep them warm.

Suddenly he became aware that Mr Sleuth, the lodger who seemed to have 'turned their luck', as it were, was walking along on the opposite side of the solitary street.

Mr Sleuth's tall, thin figure was rather bowed, his head bent toward the ground. His right arm was thrust into his long Inverness cape; the other occasionally sawed the air, doubtless in order to help him keep warm. He was walking rather quickly. It was clear that he had not yet become aware of the proximity of his landlord.

Bunting felt pleased to see his lodger; it increased his feeling of general satisfaction. Strange, was it not, that that odd, peculiar-looking figure should have made all the difference to his (Bunting's) and Mrs Bunting's happiness and comfort in life?

Naturally, Bunting saw far less of the lodger than did Mrs Bunting. Their gentleman had made it very clear that he did not like either the husband or wife to come up to his rooms without being definitely asked to do so, and Bunting had been up there only once since Mr Sleuth's arrival five weeks before. This seemed to be a good opportunity for a little genial conversation.

Bunting, still an active man for his years, crossed the road, and, stepping briskly forward, tried to overtake Mr Sleuth; but the more he hurried, the more the other hastened, and that without even turning to see whose steps he heard echoing behind him on the now freezing pavement.

Mr Sleuth's own footsteps were quite inaudible—an odd circumstance, when you came to think of it, as Bunting did think of it later, lying awake by Ellen's side in the pitch-darkness. What it meant was, of course, that the lodger had rubber soles on his shoes.

The two men, the pursued and the pursuer, at last turned into the Marylebone Road. They were now within a hundred yards of home; and so, plucking up courage, Bunting called out, his voice echoing freshly on the still air:

'Mr Sleuth, sir! Mr Sleuth!'

The lodger stopped and turned round. He had been walking so quickly, and he was in so poor a physical condition, that the sweat was pouring down his face.

'Ah! So it's you, Mr Bunting? I heard footsteps behind me, and I hurried on. I wish I'd known that it was only you; there are so many queer characters about at night in London.'

'Not on a night like this, sir. Only honest folk who have business out of doors would be out such a night as this. It is cold, sir!' And then into Bunting's slow and honest mind there suddenly crept the query as to what Mr Sleuth's own business out could be on this cold, bitter night.

'Cold?' the lodger repeated. 'I can't say that I find it cold, Mr Bunting. When the snow falls the air always becomes milder.'

'Yes, sir; but tonight there's such a sharp east wind. Why, it freezes the very marrow in one's bones!'

Bunting noticed that Mr Sleuth kept his distance in a rather strange way: he walked at the edge of the pavement, leaving the rest of it, on the wall side, to his landlord.

'I lost my way,' he said abruptly. 'I've been over Primrose Hill to see a friend of mine, and then, coming back, I lost my way.'

Bunting could well believe that, for when he had first noticed Mr Sleuth he was coming from the east, and not, as he should have done if walking home from Primrose Hill, from the north.

They had now reached the little gate that gave on to the shabby, paved court in front of the house. Mr Sleuth was walking up the flagged path, when, with a 'By your leave, sir,' the ex-butler, stepping aside, slipped in front of his lodger, in order to open the front door for him.

As he passed by Mr Sleuth, the back of Bunting's bare left hand brushed lightly against the long Inverness cape the other man was wearing, and, to his surprise, the stretch of cloth against which his hand lay for a moment was not only damp, damp from the flakes of snow that had settled upon it, but wet—wet and gluey. Bunting thrust his left hand into his pocket; it was with the other that he placed the key in the lock of the door.

The two men passed into the hall together. The house seemed blackly dark in comparison with the lighted-up road outside; and then, quite suddenly, there came over Bunting a feeling of mortal terror, an instinctive knowledge that some terrible and immediate danger was near him. A voice—the voice of his first wife, the long-dead girl to whom his mind so seldom reverted nowadays—uttered in his ear the words, 'Take care!'

'I'm afraid, Mr Bunting, that you must have felt something dirty, foul, on my coat? It's too long a story to tell you now, but I brushed up against a dead animal—a dead rabbit lying across a bench on Primrose Hill.'

Mr Sleuth spoke in a very quiet voice, almost in a whisper.

'No, sir; no, I didn't notice nothing. I scarcely touched you, sir.' It seemed as if a power outside himself compelled Bunting to utter these lying words. 'And now, sir, I'll be saying goodnight to you,' he added.

He waited until the lodger had gone upstairs, and then he turned into his own sitting-room. There he sat down, for he felt very queer. He did not draw his left hand out of his pocket till he heard the other man moving about in the room above. Then he lit the gas and held up his left hand; he put it close to his face. It was flecked, streaked with blood.

He took off his boots, and then, very quietly, he went into the room where his wife lay asleep. Stealthily, he walked across to the toilet-table, and dipped his hand into the water-jug.

The next morning Mr Sleuth's landlord awoke with a start; he felt curiously heavy about the limbs and tired about the eyes.

Drawing his watch from under his pillow, he saw that it was nearly nine o'clock. He and Ellen had overslept. Without waking her, he got out of bed and pulled up the blind. It was snowing heavily, and, as is the way when it snows, even in London, it was strangely, curiously still.

After he had dressed he went out into the passage. A newspaper and a letter were lying on the mat. Fancy having slept through the postman's knock! He picked them both up and went into the sitting-room; then he carefully shut the door behind him, and, tossing the letter aside, spread the newspaper wide open on the table and bent over it.

As Bunting at last looked up and straightened himself, a look of inexpressible relief shone upon his stolid face. The item of news he had felt certain would be there, printed in big type on the middle sheet, was not there.

He folded the paper and laid it on a chair, and then eagerly took up his letter.

> Dear Father [it ran]: I hope this finds you as well as it leaves me. Mrs Puddle's youngest child has got scarlet fever, and aunt thinks I had better come away at once,

just to stay with you for a few days. Please tell Ellen I won't give her no trouble.

> Your loving daughter,
> Daisy

Bunting felt amazingly light-hearted; and, as he walked into the next room, he smiled broadly.

'Ellen,' he cried out, 'here's news! Daisy's coming today. There's scarlet fever in their house, and Martha thinks she had better come away for a few days. She'll be here for her birthday!'

Mrs Bunting listened in silence; she did not even open her eyes. 'I can't have the girl here just now,' she said shortly; 'I've got just as much as I can manage to do.'

But Bunting felt pugnacious, and so cheerful as to be almost light-headed. Deep down in his heart, he looked back to last night with a feeling of shame and self-rebuke. Whatever had made such horrible thoughts and suspicions come into his head?

'Of course Daisy will come here,' he said shortly. 'If it comes to that, she'll be able to help you with the work, and she'll brisk us both up a bit.'

Rather to his surprise, Mrs Bunting said nothing in answer to this, and he changed the subject abruptly. 'The lodger and me came in together last night,' he observed. 'He's certainly a funny kind of gentleman. It wasn't the sort of night one would choose to go for a walk over Primrose Hill, and yet that was what he had been doing—so he said.'

It stopped snowing about ten o'clock, and the morning wore itself away.

Just as twelve was striking, a four-wheeler drew up to the gate. It was Daisy—pink-cheeked, excited, laughing-eyed Daisy, a sight to gladden any father's heart. 'Aunt said I was to have a cab if the weather was bad,' she said.

There was a bit of a wrangle over the fare. King's Cross, as all the world knows, is nothing like two miles from the Marylebone Road, but the man clamoured for one-and-sixpence, and hinted darkly that he had done the young lady a favour in bringing her at all.

While he and Bunting were having words, Daisy, leaving them to it, walked up the path to the door where her stepmother was awaiting her.

Suddenly there fell loud shouts on the still air. They sounded strangely eerie, breaking sharply across the muffled, snowy air. 'What's that?' said Bunting, with a look of startled fear. 'Why, whatever's that?'

The cabman lowered his voice: 'Them are crying out that 'orrible affair at King's Cross. He's done for two of 'em this time! That's what I meant when I said I might have got a better fare; I wouldn't say anything before Missy there, but folk 'ave been coming from all over London—like a fire; plenty of toffs, too. But there—there's nothing to see now!'

'What! Another woman murdered last night?' Bunting felt and looked convulsed with horror.

The cabman stared at him, surprised. 'Two of 'em, I tell yer—within a few yards of one another. He 'ave got a nerve—'

'Have they caught him?' asked Bunting perfunctorily.

'Lord, no! They'll never catch 'im! It must 'ave happened hours and hours ago—they was both stone-cold. One each end of an archway. That's why they didn't see 'em before.'

The hoarse cries were coming nearer and nearer—two news vendors trying to outshout each other.

''Orrible discovery near King's Cross!' they yelled exultantly. And as Bunting, with his daughter's bag in his hand, hurried up the path and passed through his front door, the words pursued him like a dreadful threat.

Angrily, he shut out the hoarse, insistent cries. No, he had no wish to buy a paper. That kind of crime wasn't fit reading for a young girl, such a girl as was his Daisy, brought up as carefully as if she had been a young lady by her strict Methody aunt.

As he stood in his little hall, trying to feel 'all right' again, he could hear Daisy's voice—high, voluble, excited—giving her stepmother a long account of the scarlet-fever case to which she owed her presence in London. But, as Bunting pushed open the door of the sitting-room there came a note of sharp alarm in his daughter's voice, and he heard her say: 'Why, Ellen! Whatever is the matter? You do look bad!' and his wife's muffled answer: 'Open the window—do.'

Rushing across the room, Bunting pushed up the sash. The newspaper-sellers were now just outside the house. 'Horrible discovery near King's Cross—a clue to the murderer!' they yelled. And then, helplessly, Mrs Bunting began to laugh. She laughed and laughed and laughed, rocking herself to and fro as if in an ecstasy of mirth.

'Why, father, whatever's the matter with her?' Daisy looked quite scared.

'She's in 'sterics—that's what it is,' he said shortly. 'I'll just get the water-jug. Wait a minute.'

Bunting felt very put out, and yet glad, too, for this queer seizure of Ellen's almost made him forget the sick terror with which he had been possessed a moment before. That he and his wife should be obsessed by the same fear, the same terror, never crossed his simple, slow-working mind.

The lodger's bell rang. That, or the threat of the water-jug, had a magical effect on Mrs Bunting. She rose to her feet, still trembling, but composed.

As Mrs Bunting went upstairs, she felt her legs trembling under her, and put out a shaking hand to clutch at the bannister for support. She waited a few minutes on the landing, and then knocked at the door of her lodger's parlour.

But Mr Sleuth's voice answered her from the bedroom. 'I'm, not well,' he called out querulously; 'I think I caught a chill going out to see a friend last night. I'd be obliged if you'll bring me up a cup of tea and put it outside my door, Mrs Bunting.'

'Very well, sir.'

Mrs Bunting went downstairs and made her lodger a cup of tea over the gas-ring, Bunting watching her the while in heavy silence.

During their midday dinner, the husband and wife had a little discussion as to where Daisy should sleep. It had already been settled that a bed should be made up for her in the sitting-room, but Bunting saw reason to change this plan. As the two women were clearing away the dishes, he looked up and said shortly: 'I think 'twould be better if Daisy were to sleep with you, Ellen and I were to sleep in the sitting-room.'

Ellen acquiesced quietly.

Daisy was a good-natured girl; she liked London, and wanted to make herself useful to her stepmother. 'I'll wash up; don't you bother to come downstairs,' she said.

Bunting began to walk up and down the room. His wife gave him a furtive glance; she wondered what he was thinking about.

'Didn't you get a paper?' she said at last.

'There's the paper,' he said crossly, 'the paper we always do take in, the *Telegraph*.' His look challenged her to a further question.

'I thought they were shouting something in the street—I mean, just before I took bad.'

But he made no answer; instead, he went to the top of the staircase and called out sharply: 'Daisy! Daisy, child, are you there?'

'Yes, father,' she answered from below.

'Better come upstairs out of that cold kitchen.'

He came back into the sitting-room again.

'Ellen, is the lodger in? I haven't heard him moving about. I don't want Daisy to be mixed up with him.'

'Mr Sleuth is not well today,' his wife answered; 'he is remaining in bed a bit. Daisy needn't have anything to do with him. She'll have her work cut out looking after things down here. That's where I want her to help me.'

'Agreed,' he said.

When it grew dark, Bunting went out and bought an evening paper. He read it out of doors in the biting cold, standing beneath a street lamp. He wanted to see what was the clue to the murderer.

The clue proved to be a very slender one—merely the imprint in the snowy slush of a half-worn rubber sole; and it was, of course, by no means certain that the sole belonged to the boot or shoe of the murderer of the two doomed women who had met so swift and awful a death in the arch near King's Cross station. The paper's special investigator pointed out that there were thousands of such soles being worn in London. Bunting found comfort in that obvious fact. He felt grateful to the special investigator for having stated it so clearly.

As he approached his house, he heard curious sounds coming from the inner side of the low wall that shut off the courtyard from the pavement. Under ordinary circumstances Bunting would have gone at once to drive whoever was there out into the roadway. Now he stayed outside, sick with suspense and anxiety. Was it possible that their place was being watched—already?

But it was only Mr Sleuth. To Bunting's astonishment, the lodger suddenly stepped forward from behind the wall on to the flagged path. He was carrying a brown-paper parcel, and, as he walked along, the new boots he was wearing creaked and the tap-tap of wooden heels rang out on the stones.

Bunting, still hidden outside the gate, suddenly understood what his lodger had been doing the other side of the wall, Mr Sleuth had been out to buy himself a pair of boots, and had gone inside the gate to put them on, placing his old footwear in the paper in which the new boots had been wrapped.

Bunting waited until Mr Sleuth had let himself into the house; then he also walked up the flagged pathway, and put his latch-key in the door.

In the next three days, each of Bunting's waking hours held its mind of aching fear and suspense. From his point of view, almost any alternative would be preferable to that which to most people would have seemed the only one open to him. He told himself that it would be ruin for him and for his Ellen to be mixed up publicly in such a terrible affair. It would track them to their dying day.

Bunting was also always debating within himself as to whether he should tell Ellen of his frightful suspicion. He could not believe that what had become so plain to himself could long be concealed from all the world, and yet lie did not credit his wife with the same intelligence. He did not even notice that, although she waited on Mr Sleuth as assiduously as ever, Mrs Bunting never mentioned the lodger.

Mr Sleuth, meanwhile, kept upstairs, he had given up going out altogether. He still felt, so he assured his landlady, far from well.

Daisy was another complication, the more so that the girl, whom her father longed to send away and whom he would hardly let out of his sight, showed herself inconveniently inquisitive concerning the lodger.

'Whatever does he do with himself all day?' she asked her stepmother.

'Well, just now he's reading the Bible,' Mrs Bunting had answered, very shortly and dryly.

'Well, I never! That's a funny thing for a gentleman to do!' Such had been Daisy's pert remark, and her stepmother had snubbed her well for it.

3

Daisy's eighteenth birthday dawned uneventfully. Her father gave her what he had always promised she should have on her eighteenth birthday—a watch. It was a pretty little silver watch, which Bunting had bought second-hand on the last day he had been happy; it seemed a long time ago now.

Mrs Bunting thought a silver watch was a very extravagant present, but she had always had the good sense not to interfere between her husband and his child. Besides, her mind was now full of other things. She was beginning to fear that Bunting suspected something, and she was filled with watchful anxiety and unease. What if he were to do anything silly—mix him up with the police, for instance? It certainly would be ruination to them both. But there—one never knew, with men! Her husband, however, kept his own counsel absolutely.

Daisy's birthday was on Saturday. In the middle of the morning, Ellen and Daisy went down into the kitchen. Bunting didn't like the feeling that there was only one flight of stairs between Mr Sleuth and himself, so he quietly slipped out of the house and went to buy himself an ounce of tobacco.

In the last four days Bunting had avoided his usual haunts. But, today, the unfortunate man had a curious longing for human companionship—companionship, that is, other than that of Ellen and Daisy. This feeling led him into a small, populous thoroughfare hard by the Edgeware Road. There were more people there than usual, for the housewives of the neighbourhood were doing their marketing for Sunday.

Bunting passed the time of day with the tobacconist, and the two fell into desultory talk. To the ex-butler's surprise, the man said nothing at all to him on the subject of which all the neighbourhood must still be talking.

And then, quite suddenly, while still standing by the counter, and before he had paid for the packet of tobacco he held in his hand, Bunting, through the open door, saw, with horrified surprise, that his wife was standing outside a green-grocer's shop just opposite. Muttering a word of apology, he rushed out of the shop and across the road.

'Ellen!' he gasped hoarsely. 'You've never gone and left my little girl alone in the house?'

Mrs Bunting's face went chalky white. 'I thought you were indoors,' she said. 'You *were* indoors. Whatever made you come out for, without first making sure I was there?'

Bunting made no answer; but, as they stared at each other in exasperated silence, *each knew that the other knew*.

They turned and scurried down the street.

'Don't run,' he said suddenly; 'we shall get there just as quickly if we walk fast. People are noticing you, Ellen. Don't run.'

He spoke breathlessly, but it was breathlessness induced by fear and excitement, not by the quick pace at which they were walking.

As last they reached their own gate. Bunting pushed past in front of his wife. After all, Daisy was his child—Ellen couldn't know how he was feeling. He made the path almost in one leap, and fumbled for a moment with his latch-key. The door opened.

'Daisy!' he called out in a wailing voice. 'Daisy, my dear, where are you?'

'Here I am, father; what is it?'

'She's all right!' Bunting turned his grey face to his wife, 'She's all right, Ellen!' Then he waited a moment, leaning against the wall of the passage. 'It did give me a turn,' he said; and then, warningly, 'Don't frighten the girl, Ellen.'

Daisy was standing before the fire in the sitting-room, admiring herself in the glass. 'Oh, father,' she said, without turning round, 'I've seen the lodger! He's quite a nice gentleman—though, to be sure, he does look queer! He came down to ask Ellen for something, and we had quite a nice little chat. I told him it was my birthday, and he asked me to go to Madame Tussaud's with him this afternoon.' She laughed a little self-consciously. 'Of course I could see he was 'centric, and then at first he spoke so funnily. "And who be you?" he said, threatening-like. And I said to him, "I'm Mr Bunting's daughter, sir."'

'"Then you're a very fortunate girl"—that's what he said, Ellen—"to 'ave such a nice stepmother as you've got. That's why," he said, "you look such a good, innocent girl." And then he quoted a bit of the prayer-book at me. "Keep innocency," he said, wagging his head at me. Lor'! It made me feel as if I was with aunt again.'

'I won't have you going out with the lodger—that's flat.' He was wiping his forehead with one hand, while with the other, he mechanically squeezed the little packet of tobacco, for which, as he now remembered, he had forgotten to pay.

Daisy pouted. 'Oh, father, I think you might let me have a treat on my birthday! I told him Saturday wasn't a very good day—at least, so I'd heard—for Madame Tussaud's. Then he said we could go early, while the fine folk are still having their dinners. He wants you to come, too.' She turned to her stepmother, then giggled happily. 'The lodger has a wonderful fancy for you, Ellen; if I was father, I'd feel quite jealous!'

Her last words were cut across by a loud knock on the door. Bunting and his wife looked at each other apprehensively.

Both felt a curious thrill of relief when they saw that it was only Mr Sleuth—Mr Sleuth dressed to go out: the tall hat he had worn when he first came to them was in his hand, and he was wearing a heavy overcoat.

'I saw you had come in'—he addressed Mrs Bunting in his high, whistling, hesitating voice, '—and so I've come down to ask if you and Miss Bunting will come to Madame Tussaud's now. I have never seen these famous waxworks, though I've heard of the place all my life.'

As Bunting forced himself to look fixedly at his lodger, a sudden doubt, bringing with it a sense of immeasurable relief, came to him. Surely it was inconceivable that this gentle, mild-mannered gentleman could be the monster of cruelty and cunning that Bunting had but a moment ago believed him to be!

'You're very kind, sir, I'm sure.' He tried to catch his wife's eye, but Mrs Bunting was looking away, staring into vacancy. She still, of course, wore the bonnet and cloak in which she had just been out to do her marketing. Daisy was already putting on her hat and coat.

Madame Tussaud's had hitherto held pleasant memories for Mrs Bunting. In the days when she and Bunting were courting they often spent part of their 'afternoon out' there. The butler had an acquaintance, a man named Hopkins, who was one of the waxworks' staff, and this man had sometimes given him passes for 'self and lady'. But this was the first time Mrs Bunting had been inside the place since she had come to live almost next door, as it were, to the big building.

The ill-sorted trio walked up the great staircase and into

the first gallery; and there Mr Sleuth suddenly stopped short. The presence of those curious, still figures, suggesting death in life, seemed to surprise and affright him.

Daisy took quick advantage of the lodger's hesitation and unease.

'Oh, Ellen,' she cried, 'do let us begin by going into the Chamber of Horrors! I've never been in there. Aunt made father promise he wouldn't take me, the only time I've ever been here. But now that I'm eighteen I can do just as I like; besides, aunt will never know!'

Mr Sleuth looked down at her.

'Yes,' he said, 'let us go into the Chamber of Horrors; that's a good idea, Miss Bunting.'

They turned into the great room in which the Napoleonic relics are kept, and which leads into the curious, vault-like chamber where waxen effigies of dead criminals stand grouped in wooden docks. Mrs Bunting was at once disturbed and relieved to see her husband's old acquaintance, Mr Hopkins, in charge of the turnstile admitting the public to the Chamber of Horrors.

'Well, you are a stranger,' the man observed genially. 'I do believe this is the very first time I've seen you in here, Mrs Bunting, since you married!'

'Yes,' she said; 'that is so. And this is my husband's daughter, Daisy; I expect you've heard of her, Mr Hopkins. And this,' she hesitated a moment, 'is our lodger, Mr Sleuth.'

But Mr Sleuth frowned and shuffled away. Daisy, leaving her stepmother's side, joined him.

Mrs Bunting put down three sixpences.

'Wait a minute,' said Hopkins; 'you can't go into the Chamber of Horrors just yet. But you won't have to wait more than four or five minutes, Mrs Bunting. It's this way, you see; our boss is in there, showing a party round.' He lowered his voice. 'It's Sir John Burney—I suppose you know who Sir John Burney is?'

'No,' she answered indifferently; 'I don't know that I ever heard of him.' She felt slightly—oh, very slightly—uneasy about Daisy. She would like her stepdaughter to keep well within sight and sound. Mr Sleuth was taking the girl to the other end of the room.

'Well, I hope you never *will* know him—not in any personal sense, Mrs Bunting.' The man chuckled. 'He's the Head Commissioner of Police—that's what Sir John Burney is. One of the gentlemen he's showing round our place is the Paris Prefect of Police, whose job is on all fours, so to speak, with Sir John's. The Frenchy has brought his daughter with him, and there are several other ladies. Ladies always like 'orrors, Mrs Bunting; that's our experience here. "Oh, take me to the Chamber of 'Orrors!"—that's what they say the minute they get into the building.'

A group of people, all talking and laughing together, were advancing from within toward the turnstile.

Mrs Bunting stared at them nervously. She wondered which of them was the gentleman with whom Mr Hopkins had hoped she would never be brought into personal contact. She quickly picked him out. He was a tall, powerful, nice-looking gentleman with a commanding manner. Just now he was smiling down into the face of a young lady. 'Monsieur Barberoux is quite right,' he was saying; 'the English law is too kind to the criminal, especially to the murderer. If we conducted our trials in the French fashion, the place we have just left would be very much fuller than it is today! A man of whose guilt we are absolutely assured is oftener than not acquitted, and then the public taunt us with "another undiscovered crime"!'

'D'you mean, Sir John, that murderers sometimes escape scot-free? Take the man who has been committing all those awful murders this last month. Of course, I don't know much about it, for father won't let me read about it, but I can't help being interested!' Her girlish voice rang out, and Mrs Bunting heard every word distinctly.

The party gathered round, listening eagerly to hear what the Head Commissioner would say next.

'Yes.' He spoke very deliberately. 'I think we may say—now, don't give me away to a newspaper fellow, Miss Rose—that we do know perfectly well who the murderer in question is—'

Several of those standing nearby uttered expressions of surprise and incredulity.

'Then why don't you catch him?' cried the girl indignantly.

'I didn't say we know where he is; I only said we know who he is; or, rather, perhaps I ought to say that we have a very strong suspicion of his identity.'

Sir John's French colleague looked up quickly. 'The Hamburg and Liverpool man?' he said interrogatively.

The other nodded. 'Yes; I suppose you've had the case turned up?'

Then, speaking very quickly, as if he wished to dismiss the subject from his own mind and from that of his auditors, he went on:

'Two murders of the kind were committed eight years ago— one in Hamburg, the other just afterward in Liverpool, and there were certain peculiarities connected with the crimes which made it clear they were committed by the same hand. The perpetrator was caught, fortunately for us red-handed, just as he was leaving the house of his victim, for in Liverpool the murder was committed in a house. I myself saw the unhappy man—I say unhappy, for there is no doubt at all that he was mad,'—he hesitated, and added in a lower tone—'suffering from an acute form of religious mania. I myself saw him, at some length. But now comes the really interesting point. Just a month ago this criminal, lunatic as we must regard him, made his escape from the asylum where he was confined. He arranged the whole thing with extraordinary cunning and intelligence, and we should probably have caught him long ago were it not that he managed, when on his way out of the place, to annex a considerable sum of money in gold with which the wages of the staff were about to be paid.'

The Frenchman again spoke. 'Why have you not circulated a description?' he asked.

'We did that at once,' Sir John Burney smiled a little grimly,' but only among our own people. We dare not circulate the man's description among the general public. You see, we may be mistaken, after all.'

'That is not very probable!' The Frenchman smiled a satirical little smile.

A moment later the party were walking in Indian file through the turnstile, Sir John Burney leading the way.

Mrs Bunting looked straight before her. Even had she wished to do so, she had neither time nor power to warn her lodger of his danger.

Daisy and her companion were now coming down the room, bearing straight for the Head Commissioner of Police. In another moment, Mr Sleuth and Sir John Burney would be face to face.

Suddenly Mr Sleuth swerved to one side. A terrible change came over his pale, narrow face; it became discomposed, livid with rage and terror.

But, to Mrs Bunting's relief—yes, to her inexpressible relief—Sir John Burney and his friends swept on. They passed by Mr Sleuth unconcernedly, unaware, or so it seemed to her, that there was anyone else in the room but themselves.

'Hurry up, Mrs Bunting,' said the turnstile-keeper; 'you

and your friends will have the place all to yourselves.' From an official he had become a man, and it was the man in Mr Hopkins that gallantly addressed pretty Daisy Bunting. 'It seems strange that a young lady like you should want to go in and see those 'orrible frights,' he said jestingly.

'Mrs Bunting, may I trouble you to come over here for a moment?' The words were hissed rather than spoken by Mr Sleuth's lips.

His landlady took a doubtful step forward.

'A last word with you, Mrs Bunting.' The lodger's face was still distorted with fear and passion. 'Do you think you'd escape the consequences of your hideous treachery? I trusted you, Mrs Bunting, and you betrayed me! But I am protected by a higher power, for I still have work to do. Your end will be bitter as wormwood and sharp as a two-edged sword. Your feet shall go down to death, and your steps take hold on hell.' Even while Mr Sleuth was uttering these strange, dreadful words, he was looking around, his eyes glancing this way and that, seeking a way of escape.

At last his eyes became fixed on a small placard placed above a curtain. 'Emergency Exit' was written there. Leaving his landlady's side, he walked over to the turnstile. He fumbled in his pocket for a moment, and then touched the man on the arm. 'I feel ill,' he said, speaking very rapidly; 'very ill indeed! It's the atmosphere of this place. I want you to let me out by the quickest way. It would be a pity for me to faint here—especially with ladies about.' His left hand shot out and placed what he had been fumbling for in his pocket on the other's bare palm. 'I see there's an emergency exit over there. Would it be possible for me to get out that way?'

'Well, yes, sir; I think so.' The man hesitated; he felt a slight, a very slight, feeling of misgiving. He looked at Daisy, flushed and smiling, happy and unconcerned, and then at Mrs Bunting. She was very palm; but surely her lodger's sudden seizure was enough to make her feel worried. Hopkins felt the half-sovereign pleasantly tickling his palm. The Prefect of Police had given him only half a crown—mean, shabby foreigner!

'Yes, I can let you out that way,' he said at last, 'and perhaps when you're standing out in the air on the iron balcony you'll feel better. But then you know, sir, you'll have to come round to the front if you want to come in again, for those emergency doors only open outward.'

'Yes, yes,' said Mr Sleuth hurriedly; 'I quite understand! If I feel better I'll come in by the front way, and pay another shilling—that's only fair.'

'You needn't do that if you'll just explain what happened here.'

The man went and pulled the curtain aside, and put his shoulder against the door. It burst open, and the light for a moment blinded Mr Sleuth. He passed his hand over his eyes.

'Thank you,' he said; 'thank you. I shall get all right here.'

Five days later, Bunting identified the body of a man found drowned in the Regent's Canal as that of his late lodger; and, the morning following, a gardener working in the Regent's Park found a newspaper in which were wrapped, together with a half-worn pair of rubber-soled shoes, two surgical knives. This fact was not chronicled in any newspaper; but a very pretty and picturesque paragraph went the round of the press, about the same time, concerning a small box filled with sovereigns which had been forwarded anonymously to the Governor of the Foundling Hospital.

Mr and Mrs Bunting are now in the service of an old lady, by whom they are feared as well as respected, and whom they make very comfortable.

THE PERFECT MURDER

Stacy Aumonier

One evening in November two brothers were seated in a little café in the Rue de la Roquette discussing murders. The evening papers lay in front of them, and they all contained a lurid account of a shocking affair in the Landes district, where a charcoal-burner had killed his wife and two children with a hatchet. From discussing this murder in particular they went on to discussing murder in general.

'I've never yet read a murder case without being impressed by the extraordinary clumsiness of it,' remarked Paul, the younger brother. 'Here's this fellow who murders his victims with his own hatchet, leaves his hat behind in the shed, and arrives at a village hard by, with blood on his boots.'

'They lose their heads,' said Henri, the elder. 'In cases like that they are mentally unbalanced, hardly responsible for their actions.'

'Yes,' replied Paul, 'but what impresses me is—what a lot of murders must be done by people who take trouble, who leave not a trace behind.'

Henri shrugged his shoulders. 'I shouldn't think it was so easy, old boy; there's always something that crops up.'

'Nonsense! I'll guarantee there are thousands done every year. If you are living with anyone, for instance, it must be the easiest thing in the world to murder them.'

'How?'

'Oh, some kind of accident—and then you go screaming into the street, "Oh, my poor wife! Help!" You burst into tears, and everyone consoles you. I read of a woman somewhere who murdered her husband by leaving the window near the bed open at night when he was suffering from pneumonia. Who's going to suspect a case like that? Instead of that, people must always select revolvers, or knives, or go and buy poison at the chemist's across the way.'

'It sounds as though you were contemplating a murder yourself,' laughed Henri.

'Well, you never know,' answered Paul; 'circumstances might arise when a murder would be the only way out of a difficulty. If ever my time comes I shall take a lot of trouble about it. I promise you, I shall leave no trace behind.'

As Henri glanced at his brother making this remark, he was struck by the fact that there was indeed nothing irreconcilable between the idea of a murder and the idea of Paul doing it. He was a big, saturnine-looking gentleman with a sallow, dissolute face, framed in a black square beard and swathes of untidy grey hair. His profession was that of a traveller in cheap jewellery, and his business dealings were not always the straightest. Henri shuddered. With his own puny physique, bad health, and vacillating will, he was always dominated by his younger brother. He himself was a clerk in a drapery store, and he had a wife and three children. Paul was unmarried.

The brothers saw a good deal of each other, and were very intimate. But the word friendship would be an extravagant term to apply to their relationship. They were both always hard up, and they borrowed money from each other when every other source failed.

They had no other relatives except a very old uncle and aunt who lived at Chantilly. This uncle and aunt, whose name was Taillandier, were fairly well-off, but they would have little to do with the two nephews. They were occasionally invited there to dinner, but neither Paul nor Henri ever succeeded in extracting a franc out of Uncle Robert. He was a very religious man, hard-fisted, cantankerous and intolerant. His wife was a little more pliable. She was in effect an eccentric. She had spasms of generosity, during which periods both the brothers had, at times, managed to get money out of her. But these were rare occasions. Moreover, the old man kept her so short of cash that she found it difficult to help her nephews even if she desired to.

As stated, the discussion between the two brothers occurred in November. It was presumably forgotten by both of them immediately afterwards. And indeed, there is no reason to believe that it would ever have recurred, except for certain events which followed the sudden death of Uncle Robert in the February of the following year.

In the meantime, the affairs of both Paul and Henri had gone disastrously. Paul had been detected in a dishonest transaction over a paste trinket, and had just been released from a period of imprisonment. The knowledge of this had not reached his uncle before his death. Henri's wife had had another baby, and had been very ill. He was more in debt than ever.

The news of the uncle's death came as a gleam of hope in the darkness of despair. What kind of will had he left? Knowing their uncle, each was convinced that, however it was framed there was likely to be little or nothing for them. However, the old villain might have left them a thousand or two. And in any case, if the money was all left to the wife, here was a possible field of plunder. It need hardly be said that they repaired with all haste to the funeral, and even with greater alacrity to the lawyer's reading of the will.

The will contained surprises both encouraging and discouraging. In the first place, the old man had left a considerably larger fortune than anyone could have anticipated. In the second place, all the money and securities were carefully tied up, and placed under the control of trustees. There were large bequests to religious charities, whilst the residue was held in trust for his wife. But so far as the brothers were concerned the surprise came at the end. On her death this residue was still to be held in trust, but a portion of the interest was to be divided between Henri and Paul, and on their death to go to the Church. The old man had recognized a certain call of the blood after all!

They both behaved with tact and discretion at the funeral, and were extremely sympathetic and solicitous towards Aunt Rosalie, who was too absorbed with her own trouble to take much notice of them. It was only when it came to the reading of the will that their avidity and interest outraged, perhaps, the strict canons of good taste. It was Paul who managed to get it clear from the notary what the exact amount would probably be. Making allowances for fluctuations, accidents and acts of God, on the death of Mme Taillandier, the two brothers would inherit something between eight and ten thousand francs a year each. She was eighty-two and very frail.

The brothers celebrated the good news with a carouse up in Montmartre. Naturally, their chief topic of conversation was how long the old bird would keep on her perch. In any case, it could not be many years. With any luck it might be only a few weeks. The fortune seemed blinding. It would mean comfort and security to the end of their days. The rejoicings were mixed with recriminations against the old man for his stinginess. Why couldn't he have left them a lump sum down now? Why did he want to waste all this good gold on the Church? Why all this trustee business?

There was little they could do but await developments. Except that in the meantime—after a decent interval—they might try and touch the old lady for a bit. They parted, and the next day set about their business in cheerier spirits.

For a time they were extremely tactful. They made formal calls on Aunt Rosalie, inquiring after her health, and offering their services in any capacity whatsoever. But at the end of a month Henri called hurriedly one morning, and after the usual professions of solicitude asked his aunt if she could possibly lend him one hundred and twenty francs to pay the doctor who had attended his wife and baby. She lent him forty, grumbling at his foolishness at having children he could not afford to keep. A week later came Paul with a story about being robbed by a client. He wanted a hundred. She lent him ten.

When these appeals had been repeated three or four times, and received similar treatment—and sometimes no treatment at all—the old lady began to get annoyed. She was becoming more and more eccentric. She now had a companion, an angular, middle-aged woman named Mme Chavanne, who appeared like a protecting goddess. Sometimes when the brothers called, Mme Chavanne would say that Mme Taillandier was too unwell to see anyone. If this news had been true it would have been good news indeed, but the brothers suspected that it was all pre-arranged. Two years went by, and they both began to despair.

'She may live to a hundred,' said Paul.

'We shall die of old age, first,' grumbled Henri.

It was difficult to borrow money on the strength of the will. In the first place, their friends were more of the borrowing than the lending class. And, anyone who had a little was suspicious of the story, and wanted all kinds of securities. It was Paul who first thought of going to an insurance company to try to raise money on the reversionary interest. They did succeed in the end in getting an insurance company to advance them two thousand francs each, but the negotiations took five months to complete, and by the time they had insured their lives, paid the lawyer's fees and paid for the various deeds and stamps, and signed some thirty or forty forms, each man only received a little over a thousand francs, which was quickly lost in paying accrued debts and squandering the remainder. Their hopes were raised by the dismissal of Mme Chavanne, only to be lowered again by the arrival of an even more aggressive companion. The companions came and went with startling rapidity. None of them could stand for any time the old lady's eccentricity and ill-temper. The whole of the staff was always being changed. The only one who remained loyal all through was the portly cook, Ernestine. Even this may have been due to the fact that she never came in touch with her mistress. She was an excellent cook, and she never moved from the kitchen. Moreover, the cooking required by Mme Taillandier was of the simplest nature, and she seldom entertained. And, she hardly ever left her apartment. Any complaints that were made were made through the housekeeper, and the complaints and their retaliations became mellowed in the process; for Ernestine also had a temper of her own.

Nearly another year passed before what appeared to Paul to be a mild stroke of good fortune came his way. Things had been going from bad to worse. Neither of the brothers was in a position to lend a sou to the other. Henri's family was becoming a greater drag, and people were not buying Paul's trinkets.

One day, during an interview with his aunt—Paul had been trying to borrow more money—he fainted in her presence. It is difficult to know what it was about this act which affected the old lady, but she ordered him to be put to bed in one of the rooms of the villa. Possibly, she jumped to the conclusion that he had fainted from lack of food—which was not true, Paul never went without food and drink—and she suddenly realized that after all he was her husband's sister's son. He must certainly have looked pathetic, this white-faced man, well past middle age, and broken in life. Whatever it was, she showed a broad streak of compassion for him. She ordered her servants to look after him, and to allow him to remain until she countermanded the order.

Paul, who had certainly felt faint, but had quickly seized the occasion to make it as dramatic as possible, saw in this an opportunity to wheedle his way into his aunt's favours. His behaviour was exemplary. The next morning, looking very white and shaky, he visited her, and asked her to allow him to go, as he had no idea of abusing her hospitality. If he had taken up the opposite attitude she would probably have turned him out, but because he suggested going, she ordered him to stop. During daytime he went about his dubious business, but he continued to return there at night to sleep, and to enjoy a good dinner cooked by the admirable Ernestine. He was in clover.

Henri was naturally envious when he heard of his brother's good fortune. And, Paul was fearful that Henri would spoil the whole game by going and throwing a fit himself in the presence of the aunt. But this, of course, would have been too obvious and foolish for even Henri to consider seriously. And, he racked his brains for some means of inveigling the old lady. Every plan he put forth, however, Paul sat upon. He was quite comfortable himself, and he didn't see the point of his brother butting in.

'Besides,' he said, 'she may turn me out any day. Then you can have your shot.'

They quarrelled about this, and did not see each other for some time. One would have thought that Henri's appeal to Mme Taillandier would have been stronger than Paul's. He was a struggling individual, with a wife and four children. Paul was a notorious ne'er-do-well, and he had no attachments. Nevertheless, the old lady continued to support Paul. Perhaps, it was because he was a big man, and she liked big men. Her husband had been a man of fine physique. Henri was puny, and she despised him. She had never had children of her own, and she disliked children. She was always upbraiding Henri and his wife for their fecundity. Any attempt to pander to her emotions through the sentiment of childhood failed. She would not have the children in her house. And, any small acts of charity which she bestowed upon them, seemed to be done more with the idea of giving her an opportunity to inflict her sarcasm and venom upon them than out of kindness of heart.

In Paul, on the other hand, she seemed to find something slightly attractive. She sometimes sent for him, and he, all agog—expecting to get his notice to quit—would be agreeably surprised to find that, on the contrary, she had some little commission she wished him to execute. And, you may rest assured that he never failed to make a few francs out of all these occasions. The notice to quit did not come. It may be—poor deluded woman—that she regarded him as some kind of protection. He was, in any case, the only 'man' who slept under her roof.

At first she seldom spoke to him, but as time went on she would sometimes send for him to relieve her loneliness. Nothing could have been more ingratiating than Paul's manners in these knowing circumstances. He talked expansively about politics, beforehand his aunt's views, and just what she would like him to say. Her eyesight was very bad, and he would read her the news of the day, and tell her what was happening in Paris.

He humoured her every whim. He was astute enough to see that it would be foolish and dangerous to attempt to borrow money for the moment. He was biding his time, and trying to think out the most profitable plan of campaign. There was no immediate hurry. His bed was comfortable, and Ernestine's cooking was excellent.

In another year's time, he had established himself as quite one of the permanent householders. He was consulted about the servants, and the doctors, and the management of the house, everything except the control of money, which was jealously guarded by a firm of lawyers. Many a time he would curse his uncle's foresight. The old man's spirit seemed to be hovering in the dim recesses of the over-crowded rooms, mocking him. For the old lady, eccentric and foolish in many ways, kept a strict check upon her dividends. It was her absorbing interest in life, that and an old grey perroquet, which she treated like a child. Its name was Anna, and it used to walk up and down her table at mealtimes and feed off her own plate. Finding himself so firmly entrenched Paul's assurance gradually increased. He began to treat his aunt as an equal, and sometimes even to contradict her, and she did not seem to resent it.

In the meantime, Henri was eating his heart out with jealousy and sullen rage. The whole thing was unfair. He occasionally saw Paul, who boasted openly of his strong position in the Taillandier household, and he would not believe that Paul was not getting money out of the old lady as well as board and lodging. With no additional expenses, Paul was better dressed than he used to be, and he looked fatter and better in health. All—or nearly all—of Henri's appeals, although pitched in a most pathetic key, were rebuffed. He felt a bitter hatred against his aunt, his brother, and life in general. If only she would die! What was the good of life to a woman at eighty-five or six?

And, there was he—four young children, clamouring for food, and clothes, and the ordinary decent comforts. And, there was Paul, idling his days away at cafés and his nights at cabarets—nothing to do, and no responsibilities.

Meeting Paul one day, he said:

'I say, old boy, couldn't you spring me a hundred francs? I haven't the money to pay my rent next week.'

'She gives me nothing,' replied Paul.

Henri did not believe this, but it would be undiplomatic to quarrel. He said:

'Aren't there—isn't there some little thing lying about the villa you could slip in your pocket? We could sell it, see? Go shares. I'm desperately pushed.'

Paul looked down his nose. Name of a pig! Did Henri think he had never thought of that? Many and many a time, the temptation had come to him. But no; every few months people came from the lawyer's office, and the inventory of the whole household was checked. The servants could not be suspected. They were not selected without irreproachable characters. If he were suspected—well, all kinds of unpleasant things might crop up. Oh, no, he was too well off where he was. The game was to lie in wait. The old lady simply must die soon. She had even been complaining of her chest that morning. She was always playing with the perroquet. Somehow this bird got on Paul's nerves. He wanted to wring its neck. He imitated the way she would say, 'There's a pretty lady! Oh, my sweet! Another nice grape for my little one. There's a pretty lady!' He told Henri all about this, and the elder brother went on his way with a grunt that only conveyed doubt and suspicion.

In view of this position, it seemed strange that in the end, it was Paul who was directly responsible for the dénouement in the Taillandier household. His success went to his rather weak head like wine. He began to swagger and buster and abuse his aunt's hospitality. And, curiously enough, the more he advanced the further she withdrew. The eccentric old lady seemed to be losing her powers of resistance so far as he was concerned. And, he began to borrow small sums of money from her, and, as she acquiesced so readily, to increase his demands. He let his travelling business go, and sometimes he would get lost for days at a time. He would spend his time at the races, and drinking with doubtful acquaintances in obscure cafés. Sometimes he won, but in the majority of cases he lost. He ran up bills and got into debt. By cajoling small sums out of his aunt he kept his debtors at bay for nearly nine months.

But one evening he came to see Henri in a great state of distress. His face, which had taken on a healthier glow when he first went to live with his aunt, had become puffy and livid. His eyes were bloodshot.

'Old boy,' he said, 'I'm at my wits' end. I've got to find seven thousand francs by the twenty-first of the month, or they're going to foreclose. How do you stand? I'll pay you back.'

To try to borrow money from Henri was like appealing to the desert for a cooling draught. He also had to find money by the twenty-first, and he was overdrawn at the bank. They exchanged confidences, and in their mutual distress they felt sorry for each other and for themselves. It was a November evening, and the rain was driving along the boulevards in fitful gusts. After trudging a long way they turned into a little café in the Rue de la Roquette, and sat down and ordered two cognacs. The café was almost deserted. A few men in mackintoshes were scattered around reading the evening papers. They sat at a marble table in the corner and tried to think of ways and means. But after a time, a silence fell between them. There seemed nothing more to suggest. They could hear the rain beating on the skylight. An old man, four tables away, was poring over *La Patrie*.

Suddenly, Henri looked furtively around the room and clutched his brother's arm.

'Paul!' he whispered.

'What is it?'

'Do you remember—it has all come back to me—suddenly—one night, a night something like this—it must be give or take, six years ago—we were seated here in this same café—do you remember?'

'No. I don't remember. What was it?'

'It was the night of that murder in the Landes district. We got talking about—don't you remember?'

Paul scratched his temple and sipped the cognac. Henri leant closer to him.

'You said—you said that if you lived with anyone, it was the easiest thing in the world to murder them. An accident, you know. And, you go screaming into the street—'

Paul started, and stared at his brother, who continued:

'You said that if ever you—you had to do it, you would guarantee that you would take every trouble. You wouldn't leave a trace behind.'

Paul was acting. He pretended to half-remember, to half-understand. But his eyes narrowed. Imbecile! Hadn't he been through it all in imagination a hundred times? Hadn't he already been planning and scheming an act for which his brother would reap half the benefit? Nevertheless, he was staggered. He never imagined that the suggestion would come from Henri. He was secretly relieved. If Henri was to receive half the benefit, let him also share half the responsibilities. The risk in any case would be wholly his. He grinned enigmatically, and they put their heads together. And so, in that dim corner of the café was planned the perfect murder.

Coining up against the actual proposition, Paul had long since realized that the affair was not so easy of accomplishment as he had so airily suggested. For the thing must be done without violence, without clues, without a trace. Such ideas as leaving the window open at night were out of the question, as the companion slept in the same room. Moreover, the old lady was quite capable of getting out of bed and shutting it herself if she felt a draught. Some kind of accident? Yes, but what? Suppose she slipped and broke her neck when Paul was in the room. It would be altogether too suspicious. Besides, she would probably only partially break her neck. She would regain sufficient consciousness to tell. To drown her in her bath? The door was always locked or the companion hovering around.

'You've always got to remember,' whispered Paul, 'if any suspicion falls on me, there's the motive. There's strong motive why I should—it's got to be absolutely untraceable. I don't care if some people do suspect afterwards—when we've got the money.'

'What about her food?'

'The food is cooked by Ernestine, and the companion serves it. Besides, suppose I got a chance to tamper with the food, how am I going to get hold of—you know?'

'Weed-killer?'

'Yes, I should be in a pretty position if they traced the fact that I had bought weed-killer. You might buy some and let me have a little on the quiet.'

Henri turned pale. 'No, no; the motive applies to me, too. They'd get us both.'

When the two pleasant gentlemen parted at midnight their plans were still very immature, but they arranged to meet the following evening. It was the thirteenth of the month. To save the situation the deed must be accomplished within eight days. Of course, they wouldn't get the money at once, but, knowing the circumstances, creditors would be willing to wait. When they met the following evening in the Café des Sentiers, Paul appeared flushed and excited, and Henri was pale and on edge. He hadn't slept. He wanted to wash the whole thing out.

'And, sell up your home, I suppose?' sneered Paul.

'Listen, my little cabbage. I've got it. Don't distress yourself. You proposed this last night. I've been thinking about it and watching for months. Ernestine is a good cook, and very methodical. Oh, very methodical! She does everything every day in the same way, exactly to schedule. My apartment is on the same floor, so I am able to appreciate her punctuality and exactness. The old woman eats sparingly and according to routine. One night she has fish. The next night she has a soufflé made with two eggs. Fish, soufflé, fish, soufflé, regular as the beat of a clock. Now, listen. After lunch every day, Ernestine washes up the plates and pans. After that she prepares roughly the evening meal. If it is a fish night, she prepares the fish ready to pop into the pan. If it is a soufflé night, she beats up two eggs and puts them ready in a basin. Having done that, she changes her frock, powders her nose, and goes over to the convent to see her sister who is working there. She is away an hour and a half. She returns punctually at four o'clock. You could set your watch by her movements.'

'Yes, but—'

'It is difficult to insert what I propose in fish, but I don't see any difficulty in dropping it into two beaten-up eggs, and giving an extra twist to the egg-whisk, or whatever they call it.'

Henri's face was quite grey.

'But—but—Paul, how are you going to get hold of the poison?'

'Who said anything about poison?'

'Well, but what?'

'That's where you come in.'

'Yes, you're in it, too, aren't you? You get half the spoils, don't you? Why shouldn't you—some time tomorrow when your wife's out—'

'What?'

'Just grind up a piece of glass.'

'Glass!'

'Yes, you've heard of glass, haven't you? An ordinary piece of broken wine glass will do. Grind it up as fine as a powder, the finer the better, the finer the more effective.'

Henri gasped. No, no, he couldn't do this thing. Very well, then; if he was such a coward, Paul would have to do it himself. And perhaps, when the time came Henri would also be too frightened to draw his dividends. Perhaps, he would like to make them over to his dear brother Paul? Come, it was only a little thing to do. Eight days to the twenty-first. Tomorrow, fish day, but Wednesday would be soufflé. So easy, so untraceable, so safe.

'But you,' whined Henri, 'they will suspect you.'

'Even if they do they can prove nothing. But in order to avoid this unpleasantness, I propose to leave home soon after breakfast. I shall return at a quarter-past three, letting myself in through the stable yard. The stables, as you know, are not used. There is no one else on that floor. Ernestine is upstairs. She only comes down to answer the front door bell. I shall be in and out of the house within five minutes, and I shan't return till late at night, when perhaps—I may be too late to render assistance.'

Henri was terribly agitated. On the one hand was—just murder, a thing he had never connected himself with in his life. On the other hand was comfort for himself and his family, an experience he had given up hoping for. It was in any case not exactly murder on his part. It was Paul's murder. At the same time, knowing all about it, being an accessory before the fact, it would seem contemptible to a degree to put the whole onus on Paul. Grinding up a piece of glass was such a little thing. It couldn't possibly incriminate him. Nobody could ever prove that he'd done it. But it was a terrible step to take.

'Have another cognac, my little cabbage.'

It was Paul's voice that jerked him back to actuality. He said, 'All right, yes, yes,' but whether this referred to the cognac or to the act of grinding up a piece of glass he hardly knew himself.

From that moment to twenty-four hours later, when he handed over a white packet to his brother across the same table at the Café des Sentiers, Henri seemed to be in a nightmarish dream. He had no recollection of how he had passed the time. He seemed to pass from that last cognac to this one, and the interval was a blank.

'Fish today, soufflé tomorrow,' he heard Paul chuckling. 'Brother, you have done your work well.'

When Paul went he wanted to call after him to come back, but he was frightened of the sound of his own voice. He was terribly frightened. He went to bed very late and could not sleep. The next morning he awoke with a headache, and he got his wife to telegraph to the office to say that he was too ill to come. He lay in bed all day, visualizing over and over and over again the possible events of the evening.

Paul would be caught. Someone would catch him actually putting the powder into the eggs. He would be arrested. Paul would give him away. Why did Paul say it was so easy to murder anyone if you lived with them? It wasn't easy at all. The whole thing was chock-a-block with dangers and pitfalls. Pitfalls! At half-past three he started up in bed. He had a vision of himself and Paul being guillotined side by side! He must stop it at any cost. He began to get up. Then he realized that it was already too late. The deed had been done. Paul had said that he would be in and out of the house within five minutes at three-fifteen—a quarter of an hour ago! Where was Paul? Would he be coming to see him? He was going to spend the evening out somewhere, 'returning late at night'.

He dressed feverishly. There was still time. He could call at his aunt's, rush down to the kitchen, seize the basin of beaten-up eggs, and throw them away. But where? How? By the time he got there Ernestine would have returned. She would want to know all about it. The egg mixture would be examined, analysed. God in Heaven! It was too late! The thing would have to go on, and he suffer and wait.

Having dressed, he went out after saying to his wife, 'It's all right. It's going to be all right,' not exactly knowing what he meant. He walked rapidly along the streets with no fixed destination in his mind. He found himself in the Café Rue de la Roquette, where the idea was first conceived, where he had reminded his brother.

He sat there drinking, waiting for the hours to pass.

Soufflé day, and the old lady dined at seven! It was now not quite five. He hoped Paul would turn up. A stranger tried to engage him in conversation. The stranger apparently had some grievance against a railway company. He wanted to tell him all the details about a contract for rivets, over which he had been disappointed. Henri didn't understand a word he was talking about. He didn't listen. He wanted the stranger to drop down dead or vanish into thin air. At last he called the waiter and paid for his reckoning, indicated by a small pile of saucers. From there he walked rapidly to the Café des Sentiers, looking for Paul. He was not there. Six o'clock. One hour more. He could not keep still. He paid and went on again, calling at café after café. A quarter to seven. Pray God that she threw it away. Had he ground it fine enough?

Five minutes to seven. Seven o'clock. Now. He picked up his hat and went again. The brandy had gone to his head. At half-past seven he laughed recklessly. After all, what was the good of life to this old woman of eighty-six? He tried to convince himself that he had done it for the sake of his wife and children. He tried to concentrate on the future, how he could manage on eight or ten thousand francs a year. He would give notice at the office, be rude to people who had been bullying him for years—that old blackguard Mocquin!

At ten o'clock he was drunk, torpid and indifferent. The whole thing was over for good or ill. What did it matter? He terribly wanted to see Paul, but he was too tired to care very much. The irrevocable step had been taken. He went home to bed and fell into a heavy drunken sleep.

'Henri! Henri, wake up! What is the matter with you?' His wife was shaking him. He blinked his way into a partial condition of consciousness. November sunlight was pouring into the room.

'It's late, isn't it?' he said, involuntarily.

'It's past eight. You'll be late at the office. You didn't go yesterday. If you go on like this you'll get the sack, and then what shall we do?'

Slowly the recollection of last night's events came back to him.

'There's nothing to worry about,' he said. 'I'm too ill to go today. Send them another telegram. It'll be all right.'

His wife looked at him searchingly. 'You've been drinking,' she said. 'Oh, you men! God knows what will become of us.'

She appeared to be weeping in her apron. It struck him forcibly at that instant how provoking and small women are. Here was Jeannette crying over her petty troubles. Whereas he—

The whole thing was becoming vivid again. Where was Paul? What had happened? Was it at all likely that he could go down to an office on a day like this, a day that was to decide his fate?

He groaned, and elaborated rather pathetically his imaginary ailments, anything to keep this woman quiet. She left him at last, and he lay there waiting for something to happen. The hours passed. What would be the first intimation? Paul or the gendarmes? Thoughts of the latter stirred him to a state of fevered activity. About midday he arose, dressed, and went out. He told his wife he was going to the office, but he had no intention of doing so. He went and drank coffee at a place up in the Marais. He was terrified of his old haunts. He wandered from place to place, uncertain how to act. Late in the afternoon, he entered a café in the Rue Alibert. At a kiosk outside he bought a late edition of an afternoon newspaper. He sat down, ordered a drink and opened the newspaper. He glanced at the central news page, and as his eye absorbed one paragraph he unconsciously uttered a low scream. The paragraph was as follows:

Mysterious Affair at Chantilly

A mysterious affair occurred at Chantilly this morning. A middle-aged man, named Paul Denoyel, complained of pains in the stomach after eating an omelette. He died soon after in great agony. He was staying with his aunt, Mme Taillandier. No other members of the household were affected. The matter is to be inquired into.

The rest was a dream. He was only vaguely conscious of the events which followed. He wandered through it all, the instinct of self-preservation bidding him hold his tongue in all circumstances. He knew nothing. He had seen nothing. He had a visionary recollection of a plump, weeping Ernestine, at the inquest, enlarging upon the eccentricities of her mistress. A queer woman, who would brook no contradiction. He heard a lot about the fish day and the soufflé day, and how the old lady insisted that this was a fish day and that she had had a soufflé the day before. You could not argue with her when she was like that. And, Ernestine had beaten up the eggs all ready for the soufflé—most provoking! But Ernestine was a good cook, of method and economy. She wasted nothing. What should she do with the eggs? Why, of course, Mr Paul, who since he had come to live there was never content with a *café cornplet*. He must have a breakfast, like these English and other foreigners do. She made him an omelette, which he ate heartily.

Then the beaten-up eggs with their deadly mixture were intended for Mme Taillandier? But who was responsible for this? Ernestine? But there was no motive here. Ernestine gained nothing by her mistress's death. Indeed she only stood to lose her situation. The inquiry went on a long while. Henri himself was conscious of being in the witness box. He knew nothing. He couldn't understand it. His brother would not be likely to do that. He himself was prostrate with grief. He loved his brother.

There was nothing to do but return an open verdict. Shadowy figures passed before his mind's eye—shadowy figures and shadowy realizations. He had perfectly murdered his brother. The whole of the dividends of the estate would one day be his, and his wife's and children's. Eighteen thousand francs a year! One day—

One vision more vivid than the rest—the old lady on the day following the inquest, seated bolt upright at her table, like a figure of perpetuity, playing with the old grey perroquet, stroking its mangy neck.

'There's a pretty lady! Oh, my sweet! Another nice grape for my little one. There's a pretty lady!'

THE SQUAW

Bram Stoker

Nurnberg at the time was not so much exploited as it has been since then. Irving had not been playing *Faust*, and the very name of the old town was hardly known to the great bulk of the travelling public. My wife and I being in the second week of our honeymoon naturally wanted someone else to join our party, so that when the cheery stranger, Elias P. Hutcheson, hailing from Isthmian City, Bleeding Gulch, Maple Tree County, Neh., turned up at the station at Frankfort, and casually remarked that he was going on to see the most all-fired old Methusaleh of a town in Yurrup, and that he guessed that so much travelling alone was enough to send an intelligent, active citizen into the melancholy ward of a daft house, we took the pretty broad hint and suggested that we should join forces. We found, on comparing notes afterwards, that we had each intended to speak with some diffidence or hesitation so as not to appear too eager, such not being a good compliment to the success of our married life; but the effect was entirely marred by both of us beginning to speak at the same instant—stopping simultaneously and then going on together again. Anyhow, no matter how, it was done; and Elias P. Hutcheson became one of our party. Straightaway Amelia and I found the pleasant benefit; instead of quarrelling, as we had been doing, we found that the restraining influence of a third party was such that we now took every opportunity of spooning in odd corners. Amelia declares that ever since she has, as a result of that experience, advised all her friends to take a friend on the honeymoon. Well, we 'did' Nurnberg together, and much enjoyed the racy remarks of our transatlantic friend, who, from his quaint speech and his wonderful stock of adventures, might have stepped out of a novel. We kept for the last object of interest in the city to be visited, the Burg, and on the day appointed for the visit strolled round the outer wall of the city by the eastern side.

The Burg is seated on a rock dominating the town, and an immensely deep fosse guards it on the northern side. Nurnberg has been happy in that it was never sacked; had it been, it would certainly not be so spick and span perfect as it is at present. The ditch has not been used for centuries, and now its base is spread with tea-gardens and orchards, of which some of the trees are of quite respectable growth. As we wandered round the wall, dawdling in the hot July sunshine, we often paused to admire the views spread before us, and in especial the great plain covered with towns and villages and bounded with a blue line of hills, like a landscape of Claude Lorraine. From this we always turned with new delight to the city itself, with its myriad of quaint old gables and acre-wide red roofs dotted with dormer windows, tier upon tier. A little to our right rose the towers of the Burg, and nearer still, standing grim, the Torture Tower, which was, and is, perhaps, the most interesting place in the city. For centuries, the tradition of the Iron Virgin of Nurnberg has been handed down as an instance of the horrors of cruelty of which man is capable; we had long looked forward to seeing it; and here at last was its home.

In one of our pauses, we leaned over the wall of the moat and looked down. The garden seemed quite fifty or sixty feet below us, and the sun pouring into it with an intense, moveless heat like that of an oven. Beyond rose the grey, grim wall seemingly of endless height, and losing itself right and left in the angles of bastion and counterscarp. Trees and bushes crowned the wall, and above again towered the lofty houses on whose massive beauty, time has only set the hand of approval. The sun was hot and we were lazy; time was our own, and we lingered, leaning on the wall. Just below us was a pretty sight—a great black cat lying stretched in the sun, whilst round her gambolled prettily a tiny black kitten. The mother would wave her tail for the kitten to play with, or would raise her feet and push away the little one as an encouragement to further play. They were just at the foot of the wall, and Elias P. Hutcheson, in order to help the play, stooped and took from the walk a moderate-sized pebble.

'See!' he said, 'I will drop it near the kitten, and they will both wonder where it came from.'

'Oh, be careful,' said my wife; 'you might hit the dear little thing!'

'Not me, ma'am,' said Elias P. 'Why, I'm as tender as a Maine cherry tree. Lor, bless ye, I wouldn't hurt the poor pooty little critter more'n I'd scalp a baby. An' you may bet your variegated socks on that! See, I'll drop it fur away on the outside so's not to go near her!' Thus saying, he leaned over and held his arm out at full length and dropped the stone. It may be that there is some attractive force which draws lesser matters to greater; or more probably that the wall was not plumb but sloped to its base—we not noticing the inclination from above; but the stone fell with a sickening thud that came up to us through the hot air, right on the kitten's head, and shattered out its little brains then and there. The black cat cast a swift upward glance, and we saw her eyes like green fire, fixed an instant, on Elias P. Hutcheson; and then her attention was given to the kitten, which lay still with just a quiver of her tiny limbs, whilst a thin red stream trickled from a gaping wound. With a muffled cry, such as a human being might give, she bent over the kitten licking its wound and moaning. Suddenly she seemed to realize that it was dead, and again threw her eyes up at us. I shall never forget the sight, for she looked the perfect incarnation of hate. Her green eyes blazed with lurid fire, and the white, sharp teeth seemed to almost shine through the blood which dabbled her mouth and whiskers. She gnashed her teeth, and her claws stood out stark and at full length on every paw. Then she made a wild rush up the wall as if to reach us, but when the momentum ended, fell back and further added to her horrible appearance, for she fell on the kitten and rose with her black fur smeared with its brains and blood. Amelia turned quite faint, and I had to lift her back from the wall. There was a seat close by in shade of a spreading plane tree, and here I placed her whilst she composed herself Then I went back to Hutcheson, who stood without moving, looking down on the angry cat below.

As I joined him, he said:

'Wall, I guess that air the savagest beast I ever see—'cept once when an Apache squaw had an edge on a half-breed what they nicknamed "Splinters" 'cos of the way he fixed up heripapoose which he stole on a raid just to show that he appreciated the way they had given his mother the fire torture. She got that kinder look so set on her face that it jest seemed to grow there. She followed Splinters more'n three year till at last the braves got him and handed him over to her. They did say that no man, white or Injun, had ever been so long a-dying under the tortures of the Apaches. The only time I ever see her smile was when I wiped her out. I kem on the camp just in time to see Splinters pass in his checks, and he wasn't sorry to go either. He was a hard citizen, and though I never could shake with him after that papoose business—for it was bitter bad, and he should have been a white man, for he looked like one—I see he had got paid out in full. Durn me, but I took a piece of his hide from one of his skinnin' posts an' had it made into a pocket book. It's here now!' and he slapped the breast pocket of his coast.

Whilst he was speaking, the cat was continuing her frantic efforts to get up the wall. She would take a run back and then charge up, sometimes reaching an incredible height. She did not seem to mind the heavy fall which she got each time but started with renewed vigour; and at every tumble her appearance became more horrible. Hutcheson was a kind-hearted man— my wife and I had both noticed his little acts of kindness to animals as well as to persons—and he seemed concerned at the state of fury to which the cat had wrought herself.

'Wall, now!' he said, 'I du declare that that poor critter seems quite desperate. There! There! poor thing, it was all an accident—though that won't bring back your little one to you. Say! I wouldn't have had such a thing happen for a thousand! Just shows what a clumsy fool of a man can do when he tries to play! Seems I'm too darned slipper-handed to even play with a cat. Say, Colonel!'—it was a pleasant way he had to bestow titles freely—'I hope your wife don't hold no grudge against me on account of this unpleasantness. Why, I wouldn't have had it occur on no account.'

He came over to Amelia and apologized profusely, and she with her usual kindness of heart hastened to assure him that she quite understood that it was an accident. Then we all went again to the wall and looked over.

The cat missing Hutcheson's face had drawn back across the moat, and was sitting on her haunches as though ready to spring. Indeed, the very instant she saw him she did spring, and with a blind, unreasoning fury, which would have been grotesque, only that it was so frightfully real. She did not try to run up the wall, but simply launched herself at him as though hate and fury could lend her wings to pass straight through the great distance between them. Amelia, womanlike, got quite concerned and said to Elias P. in a warning voice:

'Oh! you must be very careful. That animal would try to kill you if she were here; her eyes look like positive murder.'

He laughed out jovially. 'Excuse me, ma'am,' he said, 'but I "can't help laughin". Fancy a man that has fought grizzlies an' Injuns bein' careful of bein' murdered by a cat!'

When the cat heard him laugh, her whole demeanour seemed to change. She no longer tried to jump or run up the wall, but went quietly over, and sitting again beside the dead kitten, began to lick and fondle it as though it were alive.

'See!' said I, 'the effect of a really strong man. Even that animal in the midst of her fury recognizes the voice of a master, and bows to him!'

'Like a squaw!' was the only comment of Elias P. Hutcheson, as we moved on our way round the city fosse. Every now and then we looked over the wall and each time saw the cat following us. At first she had kept going back to the dead kitten, and then as the distance grew greater, she took it in her mouth and so followed. After a while, however, she abandoned this, for we saw her following all alone; she had evidently hidden the body somewhere. Amelia's alarm grew at the cat's persistence, and more than once she repeated her warning; but the American always laughed with amusement, till finally, seeing that she was beginning to be worried, he said:

'I say, ma'am, you needn't be skcered over that cat. I go heeled, I du!' Here he slapped his pistol pocket at the back of his lumbar region. 'Why, sooner'n have you worried, I'll shoot the critter, right here, an' risk the police interferin' with a citizen of the United States for carryin' arms contrairy to regulations!' As he spoke he looked over the wall, but the cat, on seeing him, retreated with a growl into a bed of tall flowers and was hidden. He went on: 'Blest if that ar critter ain't got more sense of what's good for her than most Christians. I guess we've seen the last of her! You bet, she'll go back now to that busted kitten and have a private funeral of it, all to herself!'

Amelia did not like to say more, lest he might, in mistaken kindness to her, fulfil his threat of shooting the cat, and so we went on and crossed the little wooden bridge leading to the gateway whence ran the steep paved roadway between the Burg and the pentagonal Torture Tower. As we crossed the bridge, we saw the cat again down below us. When she saw us, her fury seemed to return and she made frantic efforts to get up the steep wall. Hutcheson laughed as he looked down at her, and said,

'Goodbye, old girl. Sorry I injured your feelin's, but you'll get over it in time! So long!' And then we passed through the long, dim archway and came to the gate of the Burg.

When we came out again after our survey of this most beautiful old place which not even the well-intentioned efforts of the Gothic restorers of forty years ago have been able to spoil—though their restoration was then glaring white—we seemed to have quite forgotten the unpleasant episode of the morning. The old lime tree with its great trunk gnarled with the passing of nearly nine centuries, the deep well cut through the heart of the rock by those captives of old, and the lovely view from the city wall whence we heard, spread over almost a full quarter of an hour, the multitudinous chimes of the city, had all helped to wipe out from our minds the incident of the slain kitten.

We were the only visitors who had entered the Torture Tower that morning—so at least said the old custodian—and as we had the place all to ourselves were able to make a minute and more satisfactory survey than would have otherwise been possible. The custodian, looking to us as the sole source of his gains for the day, was willing to meet our wishes in any way. The Torture Tower is truly a grim place, even now when many thousands of visitors have sent a stream of life, and the joy that follows life, into the place; but at the time I mention, it wore its grimmest and most gruesome aspect. The dust of ages seemed to have settled on it, and the darkness and the horror of its memories seem to have become sentient in a way that would have satisfied the Pantheistic souls of Philo or Spinoza. The lower chamber, where we entered, was seemingly, in its normal state, filled with incarnate darkness; even the hot sunlight streaming in through the door seemed to be lost in the vast thickness of the walls, and only showed the masonry rough as when the builder's scaffolding had come down, but coated with dust and marked here and there with patches of dark stain which, if walls could speak, could have given their own dread memories of fear and pain.

We were glad to pass up the dusty wooden staircase, the custodian leaving the outer door open to light us somewhat on our way; for to our eyes the one long-wick'd, evil-smelling candle stuck in a sconce on the wall gave an inadequate light. When we came up through the open trap in the corner of the chamber overhead, Amelia held on to me so tightly that I could actually feel her heart beat. I must say for my own part that I was not surprised at her fear, for this room was even more gruesome than that below. Here there was certainly more light, but only just sufficient to realize the horrible surroundings of the place. The builders of the tower had evidently intended that only they who should gain the top should have any of the joys of light and prospect. There, as we had noticed from below, were ranges of windows, albeit of medieval smallness, but elsewhere in the tower were only a very few narrow slits such as were habitual in places of medieval defence. A few of these only lit the chamber, and these were so high up in the wall that from no part could the sky be seen through the thickness of the walls. In racks, and leaning in disorder against the walls, were a number of headsmen's swords, great double-handed weapons with broad blade and keen edge. Hard by were several blocks whereon the necks of the victims had lain, with here and there deep notches where the steel had bitten through the guard of flesh and shored into the wood.

Round the chamber, placed in all sorts of irregular ways, were many implements of torture which made one's heart ache to see—chairs full of spikes which gave instant and excruciating pain; chairs and couches with dull knobs whose torture was seemingly less, but which, though slower, were equally efficacious; racks, belts, boots, gloves, collars, all made for compressing at will; steel baskets in which the head could be slowly crushed into a pulp if necessary; watchmen's hooks with long handle and knife that cut at resistance—this a specialty of the old Nurnberg police system; and many, many other devices for man's injury to man. Amelia grew quite pale with the horror of things, but fortunately did not faint, for being a little overcome she sat down on a torture chair, but jumped up again with a shriek, all tendency to faint gone. We both pretended that it was the injury done to her dress by the dust of the chair and the rusty spikes which had upset her, and Mr Hutcheson acquiesced in accepting the explanation with a kind-hearted laugh.

But the central object in the whole of this chamber of horrors was the engine known as the Iron Virgin, which stood near the centre of the room. It was a rudely-shaped figure of a woman, something of the bell order, or, to make a closer comparison, of the figure of Mrs Noah in the children's Ark, but without that slimness of waist and perfect *rondeur* of hip which marks the aesthetic type of the Noah family. One would hardly have recognized it as intended for a human figure at all, had not the founder shaped on the forehead a rude semblance of a woman's face. This machine was coated with rust without, and covered with dust; a rope was fastened to a ring in the front of the figure, about where the waist should have been, and was drawn through a pulley, fastened on the wooden pillar which sustained the flooring above. The custodian pulling this rope showed that a section of the front was hinged like a door at one side; we then saw that the engine was of considerable thickness, leaving just room enough inside for a man to be placed. The door was of equal thickness and of great weight, for it took the custodian all his strength, aided though he was by the contrivance of the pulley, to open it. This weight was partly due to the fact that the door was of manifest purpose hung so as to throw its weight downwards, so that it might shut of its own accord when the strain was released.

The inside was honeycombed with rust—nay more, the rust alone that comes through time would hardly have eaten so deep into the iron walls; the rust of the cruel stains was deep indeed! It was only, however, when we came to look at the inside of the door that the diabolical intention was manifest to the full. Here were several long spikes, square and massive, broad at the base and sharp at the points, placed in such a position that when the door should close, the upper ones would pierce the eyes of the victim and the lower ones his heart and vitals. The sight was too much for poor Amelia, and this time she fainted dead off, and I had to carry her down the stairs and place her on a bench outside till she recovered. That she felt it to the quick was afterwards shown by the fact that my eldest son bears to this day a rude birthmark on his breast, which has, by family consent, been accepted as representing the Nurnberg Virgin.

When we got back to the chamber, we found Hutcheson still opposite the Iron Virgin; he had been evidently philosophizing, and now gave us the benefits of this thought in the shape of a sort of exordium.

'Wall, I guess I've been learnin' somethin' here while madam has been getting over her faint. 'Pears to me that we're a long way behind the times on our side of the big drink. We uster think out on the plains that the Injun could give us points in tryin' to make a man on comfortable; but I guess your old medieval law-and-order party could raise him every time. Splinters was pretty good in his bluff on the squaw, but this here young miss held a straight flush all high on him. The points of them spikes air sharp enough still, though even the edges air eaten out by what uster be on them. It'd be a good thing for our Indian section to get some specimens of this here play-toy to send round to the Reservations jest to knock the stuffin' out of the bucks, and the squaws too, by showing them as how old civilization lays over them at their best. Guess but I'll get in that box a minute jest to see how it feels!'

'Oh no! No!' said Amelia. 'It is too terrible!'

'Guess, ma'am, nothin's too terrible to the explorin' mind. I've been in some queer places in my time. Spent a night inside a dead horse while a prairie fire swept over me in Montana Territory—an' another time slept inside a dead buffler when the Comanches was on the war path an' didn't keer to leave my kyard on them. I've been two days in a caved-in tunnel in the Billy Broncho gold mine in New Mexico an' was one of the four shut up for three parts of a day in the caisson what slid over on her side when we was settin' the foundations of the Buffalo Bridge. I've not funked an odd experience yet, an' I don't propose to begin now!'

We saw that he was set on the experiment, so I said, 'Well, hurry up, old man, and get through it quick!'

'All right, General,' said he, 'but I calculate we ain't quite ready yet. The gentlemen, my predecessors, what stood in that thar canister, didn't volunteer for the office—not much! And I guess there was some ornamental tyin' up before the big stroke was made. I want to go into this thing fair and square, so I must get fixed up proper first. I dare say this old galoot can rise some string and tie me up accordin' to sample?'

This was said interrogatively to the old custodian, but the latter, who understood the drift of his speech, though perhaps not appreciating to the full the niceties of dialect and imagery, shook his head. His protest was, however, only formal and made to be overcome. The American thrust a gold piece into his hand, saying, 'Take it, pard! it's your pot; and don't be skcer'd. This ain't no necktie party that you're asked to assist in!' He produced some thin frayed rope and proceeded to bind our companion with sufficient strictness for the purpose. When the upper part of his body was bound, Hutcheson said,

'Hold on a moment, Judge. Guess I'm too heavy for you to tote into the canister. You jest let me walk in, and then you can wash up regardin' my legs!'

Whilst speaking he had backed himself into the opening which was just enough to hold him. It was a close fit and no mistake. Amelia looked on with fear in her eyes, but she evidently did not like to say anything. Then the custodian completed his task by tying the American's feet together so that he was now absolutely helpless and fixed in his voluntary prison. He seemed to really enjoy it, and the incipient smile which was habitual to his face blossomed into actuality as he said,

'Guess this here Eve was made out of the rib of a dwarf! There ain't much room for a full-grown citizen of the United States to hustle. We uster make our coffins more roomier in Idaho territory. Now, Judge, you jest begin to let this door down, slow, on to me. I want to feel the same pleasure as the other jays had when those spikes began to move toward their eyes!'

'Oh no! No! No!' broke in Amelia hysterically. 'It is too terrible! I can't bear to see it!— I can't! I can't!'

But the American was obdurate. 'Say, Colonel,' said he, 'why not take Madame for a little promenade? I wouldn't hurt her feelin's for the world; but now that I am here, havin' kem eight thousand miles, wouldn't it be too hard to give up the very experience I've been pinin' an' pantin' fur? A man can't get to feel like canned goods every time! Me and the Judge here'll fix up this thing in no time, an' then you'll come back, an' we'll all laugh together!'

Once more the resolution that is born of curiosity triumphed, and Amelia stayed holding tight to my arm and shivering whilst the custodian began to slacken slowly inch by inch the rope that held back the iron door. Hutcheson's face was positively radiant as his eyes followed the first movement of the spikes.

'Wall!' he said, 'I guess I've not had enjoyment like this since I left Noo York. Bar a scrap with a French sailor at Wapping— an' that warn't much of a picnic neither—I've not had a show fur real pleasure in this dod-rotted continent, where there ain't no b'ars nor no Injuns, an' wheer nary man goes heeled. Slow there, Judge! Don't you rush this business! I want a show for my money this game—I du!'

The custodian must have had in him some of the blood of his predecessors in that ghastly tower, for he worked the engine with a deliberate and excruciating slowness which after five minutes, in which the outer edge of the door had not moved half as many inches, began to overcome Amelia. I saw her lips whiten, and felt her hold upon my arm relax. I looked around an instant for a place whereon to lay her, and when I looked at her again, found that her eye had become fixed on the side of the Virgin. Following its direction I saw the black cat crouching out of sight. Her green eyes shone like danger lamps in the gloom of the place, and their colour was heightened by the blood which still smeared her coat and reddened her mouth. I cried out,

'The cat! Look out for the cat!' for even then she sprang out before the engine. At this moment she looked like a triumphant demon. Her eyes blazed with ferocity, her hair bristled out till she seemed twice her normal size, and her tail lashed about as does a tiger's when the quarry is before it. Elias P. Hutcheson when he saw her was amused, and his eyes positively sparkled with fun as he said,

'Darned if the squaw hain't got on all her war paint! Jest give her a shove off if she comes any of her tricks on me, for I'm so fixed everlastingly by the boss, that durn my skin if I can keep my eyes from her if she wants them! Easy there, Judge! Don't you slack that ar rope or I'm euchered!'

At this moment Amelia completed her faint, and I had to clutch hold of her round the waist or she would have fallen to the floor. Whilst attending to her I saw the black cat crouching for a spring, and jumped up to turn the creature out.

But at that instant, with a sort of hellish scream, she hurled herself, not as we expected at Hutcheson, but straight at the face of the custodian. Her claws seemed to be tearing wildly as one sees in the Chinese drawings of the dragon rampant, and as I looked I saw one of them light on the poor man's eye and actually tear through it and down his cheek, leaving a wide band of red where the blood seemed to spurt from every vein.

With a yell of sheer terror which came quicker than even his sense of pain, the man leaped back, dropping as he did so the rope which held back the iron door. I jumped for it, but was too late, for the cord ran like lightning through the pulley-block, and the heavy mass fell forward from its own weight.

As the door closed I caught a glimpse of our poor companion's face. He seemed frozen with terror. His eyes stared with a horrible anguish, as if dazed, and no sound came from his lips.

And then the spikes did their work. Happily the end was quick, for when I wrenched open the door they had pierced so deep that they had locked in the bones of the skull through which they had crushed, and actually tore him—it—out of his iron prison till, bound as he was, he fell at full length with a sickly thud upon the floor, the face turning upward as he fell.

I rushed to my wife, lifted her up and carried her out, for I feared for her very reason if she should wake from her faint to such a scene. I laid her on the bench outside and ran back. Leaning against the wooden column was the custodian moaning in pain whilst he held his reddening handkerchief to his eyes. And sitting on the head of the poor American was the cat, purring loudly as she licked the blood which trickled through the gashed socket of his eyes.

I think no one will call me cruel because I seized one of the old executioner's swords and shore her in two as she sat.

MRS RAEBURN'S WAXWORK

Lady Eleanor Smith

The rain, which had poured with a pitiless ferocity for so long upon the chimneys and roofs of the great manufacturing city, seemed at length to enclose the whole town within towering prison walls of burnished steel. It was now afternoon; the short winter day was nearly over, and it had rained thus from dawn, would probably continue to rain throughout the night. A dark, wet dusk began to envelop the city like a sable blanket; the street-lamps sprang into life, looming ahead like the ghosts of drowned and weary daffodils, casting watery and trembling reflections upon the shining rivers that were pavements. There were few people walking the mournful streets, and those that were had to struggle and batter their way through sharp gusts of wind, bent double beneath dripping and top-heavy umbrellas.

Such a one was Patrick Lamb, and so great was his hurry that more than once as he stumbled over an unperceived kerb. He ran the risk of entangling both himself and his umbrella in the foaming, muddy torrents of the gutters beneath his feet. He had every reason to hurry; he was on his way to apply for a job, and he feared that unless he hastened he would be too late to secure this vacancy which meant so much to him.

Turning at last into a dark and narrow street, he saw opposite to him a ramshackle building of yellow brick, from the roof of which swelled forth a glass dome encrusted with the dirt and soot of ages. A flight of shallow steps led to a swing door. This was his destination.

He flung open the door and was immediately confronted by a turnstile, near which sat a seedy-looking man in an ill-fitting uniform not unlike that of a fireman.

'Sixpence, please,' said the man, and whistled through his teeth. Patrick Lamb shook his head.

'No... I'm not a visitor. I have an appointment with Mr Mugivan, the manager.'

'Ah—ha,' said the attendant knowingly, and showed him into a tiny slice of a room filled with papers, files, account books and dust. Here sat Mr Mugivan, a fat, podgy man with thick legs and a face like a tomato.

'Good afternoon,' said Patrick Lamb hesitatingly; 'I hear that you have a vacancy here for an—an attendant.'

Mr Mugivan stared for a moment at the young man's sallow, rather long face, at his deep-set grey eyes and slender, puny body.

'Who told you so?'

'My landlady, in Bury Street. She knew the last man you had here.'

'And what made you come?'

'Necessity. I'm in need of work. I was stranded here a week ago with a theatrical company.'

There was a silence. Mr Mugivan suddenly laughed, looking at his visitor rather defiantly with little red-rimmed eyes that were not unlike the eyes of a pig.

'Rather a come-down, isn't it, for an actor to find himself minding Mugivan's Waxworks?'

'That doesn't matter, sir. And, if you'll only let me, I'll

mind them damn well.'

'It's long hours,' said the proprietor, still speaking contemptuously. 'Nine in the morning till seven at night. An hour for lunch and an hour for tea. Two pounds a week—and the attendant has to wear a uniform. *An actor* wouldn't fancy that, would he?'

'Maybe I'm not an actor,' said Patrick Lamb.

Mr Mugivan spat upon the floor.

'I'll give you a trial, anyhow. What's your name?'

Patrick told him.

'Well, Lamb,' and the proprietor creaked himself out of his chair, revealing incidentally that he wore carpet slippers and had bunions, 'come with me and I'll show you Mugivan's Beauties before you go. You can start tomorrow morning.'

Obediently Patrick followed his new employer through the turnstile, which was swung round obligingly by the other attendant, down a narrow whitewashed tunnel into a large apartment.

'Ever seen figures before?' inquired Mr Mugivan.

'Waxworks? Not since I was a lad.'

'Hall of Monarchs,' said Mr Mugivan, sucking his teeth with a deprecating sound.

The room in which they found themselves was bare and vault-like; here, too, the walls were whitewashed; the floor was covered with a red drugget, and in the middle of the room was placed a sofa upholstered in shabby crimson plush. Yet, although bare, the room was not empty but crowded, crowded with a pale throng of mute and stiff and silent figures. They stood in groups, a dais to each group, and were protected from the public by a red cord which imprisoned them, like sheep in a pen, so that had they wished they could not have strayed, but must forever remain captive. There they stood and would no doubt stand throughout the ages, these tinsel kings and queens, Plantagenets and Stuarts, Tudors and Hanoverians, calm and blank and dreadfully remote, pallid of cheek and glassy of eye, indifferent to all who passed by to gape at them—a host of waxen princes, all dead, many of them forgotten, terribly isolated in their garish splendour, uncannily galvanized into a crude semblance of life that yet denied them even the elements of life, leaving them fixed, frozen and staring, while the dust thickened upon their cheap and fusty robes of purple and sham ermine.

Opposite the door through which they had come was another door leading to yet another chamber. Mr Mugivan led the way

'Curiosities and Horrors,' he explained carelessly. They passed through the second door.

Here was another room, replica of the first, but more dimly lit, more melancholy than even the Hall of Monarchs, since the illumination that winked upon this dreary scene was greenish, ghastly; such a light as might have been expected to proceed from a sconce of corpse candles. Here were more massed ranks of still, impassive figures, paler these than the monarchs in the dim grotto of their melancholy chamber, and more repellent perhaps because their stiff, indifferent bodies were clothed in the garments of everyday and borrowed no majesty from princes' robes, however sham. A skeleton gleamed white in one corner of the room, there was a stuffed ox with six legs, a tiny waxen midget and a giant of local fame. Save for these, the room was peopled only with men who had killed and who had paid the penalty for killing. A throng staring before them, expressionless, rigid, mask-like, brooding perhaps upon their cringes.

Mr Mugivan seemed more at home in the second room. He became almost conversational.

'Here's Hopkins, the Norwich strangler... Tracey, who shot a policeman... John Joseph Gilmore, cut the throats of his wife and two children...'

They moved across the room. Then, near the slit of a window, crossed by iron bars, Patrick saw her for the first time. She stood on a little dais by herself, a young woman, or, rather, the effigy of a young woman, dressed neatly in dark clothes that were already old-fashioned in cut. She carried herself proudly; like a queen, and whereas the other waxworks were completely expressionless of countenance, this one alone, with proudly curling lips and short, imperious nose, seemed, he thought, actually to live, perhaps because she was disdain incarnate. She stood there easily, gracefully, long, pale hands folded upon her breast, and Patrick, gazing, felt the cool, amused stare of her grey eyes. For a moment his heart leaped sharply; startling him, and he had a sudden impulse to move forward and look more closely at her; then this sensation was succeeded by a creeping feeling of curious discomfort. He was embarrassed; he had to avert his eyes.

'Who's that woman?' he asked impetuously, and then wished that he had not spoken.

Mr Mugivan answered him casually, with his back turned to the effigy

'That's Mrs Raeburn, the poisoner...and that's the lot, so come on.'

'Mrs Raeburn? I seem to know the name.'

'No doubt, no doubt. It was well enough known at one time.'

They walked away, towards the Hall of Monarchs, and Patrick was acutely conscious of the supercilious grey eyes that must be gazing after them. The sham eyes of a sham woman, a waxen effigy! He felt acutely ridiculous.

Mr Mugivan said no more until they found themselves once again in the little office. Then, offering Patrick a cigarette, he asked suddenly,

'You're not a fanciful sort of chap by any chance?'

'Fanciful? You mean nervous? No, I can't say that I am. Why?'

'No place for fancies, this,' confided Mr Mugivan, waving his hand in the direction of the exhibition; 'it's a lonely sort of a job most of the time, and once you start thinking the figures are looking at you, well, you're done, that's all. Last chap we had here took to having fancies. That's why you've got his job.'

Patrick felt suddenly rebellious.

'I can safely say I shan't have fancies,' he said, laughing. 'I may not be particularly brave—in fact I'm not—but I must say it would take more than a parcel of wax dolls to scare me.'

'Figures aren't dolls,' Mr Mugivan corrected, shocked.

'Figures, then,' and he thought, 'Talking of figures, that woman, Mrs Raeburn's got a good one.'

But neither he nor Mr Mugivan mentioned the name of the woman poisoner aloud.

'Nine o'clock tomorrow, then,' said Mr Mugivan.

'Nine o'clock tomorrow.'

And so they parted.

He discovered, the next day, two things about his new job. One was that his long and often lonely vigil with the waxworks gave him at times the curious and eerie sensation of being buried alive in a vault filled with the dead, the other that, with the morning, Mrs Raeburn, poisoner, had become once more a waxen effigy and was no longer a living, breathing woman. This was comforting, yet in some strange way disappointing, for it was idle to deny that he had thought of her very frequently during the course of the night, and that the prospect of meeting once more the direct gaze of her rather mocking eyes had undoubtedly stimulated him and sent him forth into the cheerless streets kindled with an eager, sparkling excitement which he rattler half-heartedly strove to suppress.

As the morning dragged by he studied a catalogue of the

exhibition, trying to memorize the many dossiers of princes and murderers. He was accustomed to learn by heart, and in three hours his task was almost complete, yet with one exception. A curious revulsion prevented him, from reading even to himself, the brief account in the catalogue of Mrs Raeburn's cringe, of discovering, through the medium of one cheap, smudged paragraph, that she had been an infamous woman, a monster of vice and cruelty. Taking a pen-knife from his pocket, he cut away from his catalogue all record of her dark deeds. Yet she remained throughout the morning a lifeless effigy and after glancing at her once, he gladly looked away.

He went out to lunch and returned for the long vigil of the afternoon. Few people came to visit the exhibition: a pair of school children in charge of a maiden aunt, two girls, who giggled and eyed him coyly, an old man, and an all amorous couple who plainly regarded his presence as a nuisance.

It was foggy outside; dusk fell early. For the first time that day as he paced the Hall of Monarchs, he became sensible of the loneliness of his position. Once again the feeling of being buried among the dead returned to him, intensified this time by a bored and brooding melancholy whereas in the morning there had also been a sense of adventure. The very tread of his feet, the only sound in the still apartment, smote lugubriously upon his ears. He would have liked to smoke, but this was, of course, forbidden.

At length he turned, and obeying an impulse which was becoming every second stronger, he moved towards the farther chamber, the Hall of Curiosities and Horrors. Here the twilight struck gloomily upon the wan and glimmering faces of the murderers, upturned to greet the first dark, smoky greyness of night; greenish they were once more, and dismal; and very hopeless in the blank resignation of their weary vigil in this dim room that was filled with the very breath of genteel decay.

He went straight towards the figure of Mrs Raeburn, standing tall and quiet and erect on her dais below the barred window. He had never been so near to her before; their eyes met, and once more she had recaptured that spark of life which had so curiously impressed him on the previous day. He gazed for some moments at her pale, clear-cut face, at her direct, ironic eyes. She appeared to return his scrutiny gravely, earnestly; scornfully; yet with a glint of interest and humour in her regard. She seemed, he thought, a woman well used to curious eyes, well able to defend herself against the stares of the inquisitive. Suddenly, to his immense astonishment, he spoke to her, and his voice rang out strangely enough in that silent room.

'I wonder what you have done?' he asked her abruptly. 'For God's sake, what can you have done that you should be here?'

There was a long pause, during the course of which he continued to examine her closely. Was it his imagination, or did her lips really curve, was there an answering twinkle in her eye? And then he turned sharply, for he had caught, or thought that he had caught, a soft, eager rustling sound from the throng of effigies behind his back. And suddenly he was saved, for two little boys came pattering in to visit the Curiosities and Horrors.

The next day saw him resolutely keeping to the Hall of Monarchs. Here, with the lifeless dummies of long dead kings, he was safe. In that other room he realized that he was in peril. And the day after, although he hungered for a glimpse of Mrs Raeburn's pale face, he still remained aloof. The next day was Saturday; with a steady stream of patrons who would have made the dankest vault seem homely and prosaic. Then Sunday, a holiday.

On Monday, he returned to the exhibition ready to laugh at himself for being a morbid fool. The rain had stopped; a feeble ray of primrose sunshine, filtering through the barred window of the second chamber, made even Mrs Raeburn seem little more than a cunningly fashioned doll of life size. And he had spoken to her, as though she were alive and could hear and understand him! He was disgusted with himself.

Yet, with the swiftly flowing dusk the murderers changed once more; assumed as was their wont with the shades of night the vivid and evil personalities they must have worn during their lifetime; seemed to stretch themselves as though released from some long spell of immobility; nodded, perhaps, to one another—even winked; perhaps brushed the dust from their shabby garments, smothered yawns, and waited, quietly expectant, for the closing of the exhibition. So Patrick thought, but it was difficult to see, for the shadows were thick in this lost and forgotten room.

He went towards the effigy of Mrs Raeburn and was not surprised to find that her eyes, alive and brilliant, almost feverish in their eager intensity; remained fixed directly upon him as though she waited to see whether he would, after his three days' absence, speak once more to her.

He was, however silent. He stared at her proud and beautiful mouth, at her long, pale hands, at the white stem of her throat, and admitted to himself that he desired her. Yet he had no immediate wish to touch her, but only longed passionately for the stiff, waxen body of this effigy to melt and transform itself into warm living flesh and blood. Somewhere, somehow, this miracle must be accomplished, for if he was unable to possess her, he thought that, such was the spell she had cast upon him, he must inevitably pine and sicken, for she was La Belle Dame Sans Merci, and he was in her thrall. At last he spoke to her, softly, scarcely knowing that he spoke.

'You are a witch,' he said, 'and you possess my body and soul. You ought to be burnt, and since you are made of wax it should not be difficult to destroy you... I have a good mind to try.'

This time there was no mistake; a gleam of sardonic laughter came to her eyes, a strange and elfin smile to her curling lips. She defied him. And as before, the row of murderers behind seemed to move simultaneously with the rustling murmur of excitement. As before, too, he was saved by a footstep from the outer world. He turned sharply, a woman came into the room.

Patrick stiffened, became once more the respectful and vigilant attendant. The woman hesitated for a moment, then approached him slowly; for she was bent and squat and elderly, and walked with the help of a stick. He noticed vaguely that she was dressed in dingy black, with a frowsy bonnet askew upon her head and a film of veil that partially concealed her face. He bent down politely.

'Yes, madam? Is there anything I can do?'

'There is,' said the old woman. Her voice was clear and decisive, the voice of one who is accustomed to command. 'I have stupidly neglected to buy a catalogue at the door, and as I am old, and not so good a walker as I was, I wonder if you would save my going back by being kind enough to tell me something about the waxworks. These are murderers, are they not?'

Patrick, only too pleased to occupy his mind in this accustomed fashion, began mechanically,

'Yes, madam. There on my right is Richard Sayers, the Scottish bodysnatcher, who shot two men before he was arrested, and protested his innocence to the last... Next to Sayers is Mugivan's conception of Jack the Ripper, the criminal who was never captured...this figure is modelled according to the description of his appearance given to the police by those persons who protested that they had seen him before or after his appalling crimes.... Next to Jack the Ripper we have Landru...'

But while his voice droned on he was dreading the moment when they must face Mrs Raeburn, when he would look once more upon her pale, remote face and meet once again her steady, contemptuous gaze. He lingered beside the midget, the freakish ox, the local giant. The old woman listened to him attentively, beady eyes darting from beneath her heavy veil. Once or twice she asked him a question, but otherwise was silent, seeming pleasantly absorbed in his monotonous catalogue of grim and fiendish crimes. At last the moment dreaded by Patrick could be postponed no longer; at last they faced the figure of Mrs Raeburn, standing slim and straight and self-possessed beneath the grating window. Suddenly Patrick remembered that he knew nothing of this murderess save that she had killed by poison; here he was speechless and could recite no bloodthirsty dossier, nor did he even know her victim; only that she was young and fair and that she had cast a spell upon him, and these things could not be told to his companion. There was a pause during the course of which the old woman examined the wax figure attentively and in silence. At length, he mumbled,

'This is Mrs Raeburn...the poisoner.'

As he spoke he shot a sharp glance at the effigy and observed that she was blank and mask-like once more, indifferent both to him and his companion. His witch had again become a waxwork.

The old lady shuffled closer to the figure, peered with a certain attentive inquisitiveness, then turned to him and remarked critically,

'The likeness is not very good.'

He was startled, and gaped, unable quite to grasp the purport of her words.

He asked, 'You knew her?'

She did not answer him, but said, still peering, 'She was

taller, she had more dignity, more of an air. And I think she was wilder. But it's long ago,' and her face changed all the time.

He asked again, trembling, his hands clammy cold, his voice unconsciously menacing, 'You knew her?'

For the first time the old creature turned to look at him, seeming to observe him closely. She chuckled, and at first he thought that one of the waxworks had laughed, so ghostly, so unexpected, was this little bubbling sound in the quietness of the dim hall.

She said, still chuckling, 'I am Mrs Raeburn.'

And as he did not answer she pulled back her veil. She was younger than he had at first supposed. She revealed a fat, gross, heavy-jowled face, sallow, unhealthy, with high Mongolian cheekbones. Her nose was squat and thick, her cheeks carved with two deep-cut lines running from her nostrils to the corners of her mouth. Her little sharp grey eyes were almost buried in folds of flesh. Beneath the shoddy bonnet a strand of hair hung untidily; it was dyed a bright orange tint. The face, which leered forth so boldly at Patrick, was seamed and stamped with the marks of every foul and obscene vice; brazen, debauched, so brutal as to be three parts animal, it seemed to hang in the air, this gargoyle face, to gloat triumphantly upon his horror and confusion. Then, swiftly, the woman whisked back her veil and said crisply, in her clear and resonant voice, 'It didn't do me justice, your image.' Then in a moment she was gone, while behind her the effigy of Mrs Raeburn, poisoner, remained standing cool and pale and remote upon her dais, all the paler, all the cooler, for being now the centre of a flood of cold and frozen moonlight.

Patrick fled after the old woman, not because he wished to see her again, but because of the two of them, the waxen image had become the more repulsive, yet, when he reached the Hall of Monarchs, she had already disappeared.

He waited, sick and shivering, until the clock struck seven and the show shut down, then he went in search of Mr Mugivan, whom he found in his office, reading an evening paper, with his feet on his desk.

'Good evening,' said Patrick. 'I want to tell you something.'

Mr Mugivan put down his paper.

'My word, young fellow, you look cheap. What is it now?'

Patrick, gulping, said, 'Do you know who's been here this afternoon?'

'I do not,' said Mr Mugivan. 'I'm proprietor of a waxwork show, not a magician. Who has been here?'

'Mrs Raeburn. The real Mrs Raeburn. She came to see her waxwork. She's just gone.'

As Mr Mugivan gaped, his red face became curiously mottled—white and purple in patches, Patrick noticed dispassionately.

'Mrs Raeburn?'

'Yes.'

Mr Mugivan climbed laboriously from his chair.

'Mrs Raeburn, eh? Somebody's been pulling your leg. You don't know your catalogue, either. Mrs Raeburn indeed?'

And he pulled a document from the untidy desk, licked his thumb, and flipped over a page.

'Mrs Raeburn,' he said, speaking very loud and not looking at Patrick, 'was scragged—hanged, you understand—hanged by the neck for the murder of her husband more than twenty years ago. That being so, you could hardly have seen her here just now. And that's enough of your funny stuff for one day.'

Patrick said nothing. There was really nothing to say. Nor did Mr Mugivan break the silence, but waddled to and fro about the little room, changing his carpet slippers for boots, struggling into his overcoat, cramming a check cap upon his head. In a moment he was gone.

Patrick switched off the office light, then went forth, as was his custom, to extinguish the gas jets in the exhibition before locking up for the night. His comrade of the turnstile had already gone home; he was alone, entirely alone, with more than a hundred waxen effigies. It was now quite dark outside, for the moon had fled behind a screen of clouds, and there was a rushing sound of strong wind, which swept in gusts past the shuttered windows.

He paused to light a forbidden cigarette, and then it was that he realized with an odd detachment that what he had seen during the afternoon was not a ghost, but something even more monstrous—a disembodied soul. The foul and evil soul of this wretched woman whose lovely image had bewitched him. The hideous reflection of a hideous mind. Behind her seeming purity and beauty had always been this horror, dormant, waiting to leap forth and devour. The wind rose, moaning, battering at the panes.

On such a night, he mused, as he tramped towards the Monarchs, ghouls would surely stalk abroad and witches soar through the air clutching their broomsticks and screaming aloud their lust for satan, vampires, sorcerers and fiends. A nightmare pack of horrors... He stretched on tiptoe to lower the gas above the wan, impassive face of King Richard II... And in the old days witches were burnt alive like the guys now consumed by flames each Fifth of November... And after burning he supposed that these evil women could do no more harm, but were destroyed for ever, they and their spells. A good job, too. He entered the second chamber.

◆

That night the inhabitants of the city were surprised to perceive a crimson flush sweeping the sky above the roof tops of a distant street. Then came a clanging of bells, a roar of motor-engines, and, hot-toot, in pursuit of the fire brigade, a yelling, excited rabble. Mugivan's Waxwork Exhibition was on fire. No one wanted to miss the show, doubly welcome because it was free.

The wind was strong that night, and licked the flames eagerly, strengthening them until the efforts of the men armed with hose-pipes became pathetic in their futility. At length the roof crashed in, and a wall of roaring flame rose as though to leap into the sky. They were triumphant, these pillars of fire, as though they knew that they were purifying, destroying a witch.

By morning Mugivan's Waxwork Show was a drenched and sooty ruin. Many of the figures were entirely destroyed, the Monarchs having been on the whole unluckier than the Murderers. Down in the Hall of Curiosities and Horrors there were a few survivors. Some were quite untouched. Mrs Raeburn, for instance, appeared to have emerged unscathed from the ordeal, and stood upon her dais proudly and gracefully, pale hands folded demurely upon her breast. And yet, on closer inspection, Mrs Raeburn proved not to be entirely unharmed.

Her waxen face had melted, and running, the stuff had twisted upon her features a strange and devilish sneer. Save for her pride of carriage she was unrecognizable, distorted. And then the firemen made a further discovery.

Lying near by, where the flames had crackled most fiercely was a charred and sodden bundle of clothing. They bent to examine it. It was, they found, a human body, the body of a young man.

THE RETURN OF IMRAY

Rudyard Kipling

> The doors were wide, the story saith,
> Out of the night came the patient wraith,
> He might not speak, and he could not stir
> A hair of the Baron's minniver—
> Speechless and strengthless, a shadow thin,
> He roved the castle to seek his kin.
> And oh,'twas a piteous thing to see
> The dumb ghost follow his enemy!
>
> *The Baron*

Imray achieved the impossible. Without warning, for no conceivable motive, in his youth, at the threshold of his career he chose to disappear from the world—which is to say, the little Indian station where he lived.

Upon a day he was alive, well, happy and in great evidence among the billiard tables at his Club. Upon a morning, he was not, and no manner of search could make sure where he might be. He had stepped out of his place; he had not appeared at his office at the proper time, and his dog cart was not upon the public roads. For these reasons, and because he was hampering, in a microscopical degree, the administration of the Indian Empire, that Empire paused for one microscopical moment to make inquiry into the fate of Imray. Ponds were dragged, wells were plumbed, telegrams were despatched down the lines of railways and to the nearest seaport town—twelve hundred miles away; but Imray was not at the end of the drag-ropes nor the telegraph wires. He was gone, and his place knew him no more.

Then the work of the great Indian Empire swept forward, because it could not be delayed, and Imray from being a man became a mystery—such a thing as men talk over at their tables in the Club for a month, and then forget utterly. His guns, horses and carts were sold to the highest bidder. His superior officer wrote an altogether absurd letter to his mother, saying that Imray had unaccountably disappeared, and his bungalow stood empty.

After three or four months of the scorching hot weather had gone by, my friend Strickland, of the Police, saw fit to rent the bungalow from the native landlord. This was before he was engaged to Miss Youghal—an affair which has been described in another place—and while he was pursuing his investigations into native life. His own life was sufficiently peculiar, and men complained of his manners and customs. There was always food in his house, but there were no regular times for meals. He ate, standing up and walking about, whatever he might find at the sideboard, and this is not good for human beings. His domestic equipment was limited to six rifles, three shotguns, five saddles, and a collection of stiff-jointed mahseer-rods, bigger and stronger than the largest salmon-rods. These occupied half of his bungalow, and the other half was given up to Strickland and his dog Tietjens—an enormous Rampur slut who devoured daily the rations of two men. She spoke to Strickland in a language of her own; and whenever, walking abroad, she saw things calculated to destroy the peace of Her Majesty the Queen–Empress, she returned to her master and laid information. Strickland would take steps at once, and the end of his labours was trouble and fine and imprisonment for other people. The natives believed that Tietjens was a familiar spirit, and treated her with the great reverence that is born of hate and fear. One room in the bungalow was set apart for her special use. She owned a bedstead, a blanket, and a drinking-trough, and if anyone came into Strickland's room at night her custom was to knock down the invader and give tongue till someone came with a light. Strickland owed his life to her, when he was on the frontier, in search of a local murderer, who came in the grey dawn to send Strickland much farther than the Andaman Islands. Tietjens caught the man as he was crawling into Strickland's tent with a dagger between his teeth; and after his record of iniquity was established in the eyes of the law he was hanged. From that date, Tietjens wore a collar of rough silver, and employed a monogram on her night-blanket; and the blanket was of double woven Kashmir cloth, for she was a delicate dog.

Under no circumstances would she be separated from Strickland; and once, when he was ill with fever, she made great trouble for the doctors, because she did not know how to help her master and would not allow another creature to attempt aid. Macarnaght, of the Indian Medical Service, beat her over her head with a gun-butt before she could understand that she must give room for those who could give quinine.

A short time after Strickland had taken Imray's bungalow, my business took me through that station, and naturally, the Club quarters being full, I quartered myself upon Strickland. It was a desirable bungalow, eight-roomed and heavily thatched against any chance of leakage from rain. Under the pitch of the roof ran a ceiling-cloth which looked just as neat as a whitewashed ceiling. The landlord had repainted it when Strickland took the bungalow. Unless you knew how Indian bungalows were built, you would never have suspected that above the cloth lay the dark three-cornered cavern of the roof, where the beams and the underside of the thatch harboured all manner of rats, bats, ants and foul things.

Tietjens met me in the verandah with a bay like the boom of the bell of St. Paul's, putting her paws on my shoulder to show she was glad to see me. Strickland had contrived to claw together a sort of meal which he called lunch, and immediately after it was finished went out about his business. I was left alone with Tietjens and my own affairs. The heat of the summer had broken up and turned to the warm damp of the rains. There was no motion in the heated air, but the rain fell like ramrods on earth, and flung up a blue mist when it splashed back. The bamboos, and the custard apples, the poinsettias, and the mango trees in the garden stood still while the warm water lashed through them, and the frogs began to sing among the aloe hedges. A little before the light failed, and when the rain was at its worst, I sat in the back verandah and heard the water roar from the eaves, and scratched myself because I was covered with the thing called prickly-heat. Tietjens came out with me and put her head in my lap and was very sorrowful; so I gave her biscuits when tea was ready, and I took tea in the back verandah on account of the little coolness found there. The rooms of the house were dark behind me. I could smell Strickland's saddlery and the oil on his guns, and I had no desire to sit among these things. My own servant came to me in the twilight, the muslin of his clothes clinging tightly to his drenched body, and told me that a gentleman had called and wished to see someone. Very much against my will, but only because of the darkness of the rooms, I went into the naked drawing room, telling my man to bring the lights. There might or might not have been a caller waiting—it seemed to me that I saw a figure by one of the windows—but when the lights came there was nothing save the spikes of the rain without, and the smell of the drinking earth in my nostrils. I explained to my servant that he was no wiser than he ought to be, and went back to the verandah to talk to Tietjens. She had gone out into the wet, and I could hardly coax her back to me; even with biscuits with sugar tops. Strickland came home, dripping wet, just before dinner, and the first thing he said was,

'Has anyone called?'

I explained, with apologies, that my servant had summoned me into the drawing room on a false alarm; or that some loafer had tried to call on Strickland, and thinking better of it had fled after giving his name. Strickland ordered dinner, without comment, and since it was a real dinner with a white tablecloth attached, we sat down.

At nine o'clock Strickland wanted to go to bed, and I was tired too. Tietjens, who had been lying underneath the table, rose up, and swung into the least exposed verandah as soon as her master moved to his own room, which was next to the stately chamber set apart for Tietjens. If a mere wife had wished to sleep out of doors in that pelting rain it would not have mattered; but Tietjens was a dog, and therefore the better animal. I looked at Strickland, expecting to see him flay her with a whip. He smiled queerly, as a man would smile after telling some unpleasant domestic tragedy. 'She has done this ever since I moved in here,' said he. 'Let her go.'

The dog was Strickland's dog, so I said nothing, but I felt all that Strickland felt in being thus made light of. Tietjens encamped outside my bedroom window, and storm after storm came up, thundered on the thatch, and died away. The lightning spattered the sky as a thrown egg spatters a barn door, but the light was pale blue, not yellow; and, looking through my split bamboo blinds, I could see the great dog standing, not sleeping, in the verandah, the hackles alift on her back and her feet anchored as tensely as the drawn wire-rope of a suspension bridge. In the very short pauses of the thunder I tried to sleep, but it seemed that someone wanted me very urgently. He, whoever he was, was trying to call me by name, but his voice was no more than a husky whisper. The thunder ceased, and Tietjens went into the garden and howled at the low moon. Somebody tried to open my door, walked about and through the house and stood breathing heavily in the verandahs, and just when I was falling asleep, I fancied that I heard a wild hammering and clamouring above my head or on the door.

I ran into Strickland's room and asked him whether he was ill, and had been calling for me. He was lying on his bed half dressed, a pipe in his mouth. 'I thought you'd come,' he said. 'Have I been walking round the house recently?'

I explained that he had been tramping in the dining room and the smoking room and two or three other places, and he laughed and told me to go back to bed. I went back to bed and slept till the morning, but through all my mixed dreams I was sure I was doing someone an injustice in not attending to his wants. What those wants were I could not tell; but a fluttering, whispering, bolt-fumbling, lurking, loitering. Someone was reproaching me for my slackness, and, half awake, I heard the howling of Tietjens in the garden and the threshing of the rain.

I lived in that house for two days. Strickland went to his office daily, leaving me alone for eight or ten hours with Tietjens for my only companion. As long as the full light lasted, I was comfortable, and so was Tietjens; but in the twilight she and

I moved into the back verandah and cuddled each other for company. We were alone in the house, but none the less it was much too fully occupied by a tenant with whom I did not wish to interfere. I never saw him, but I could see the curtains between the rooms quivering where he had just passed through; I could hear the chairs creaking as the bamboos sprung under a weight that had just quit them; and I could feel when I went to get a book from the dining room that somebody was waiting in the shadows of the front verandah till I should have gone away. Tietjens made the twilight more interesting by glaring into the darkened rooms with every hair erect, and following the motions of something that I could not see. She never entered the rooms, but her eyes moved interestedly and that was quite sufficient. Only when my servant came to trim the lamps and make all light and habitable, she would come in with me and spend her time sitting on her haunches, watching an invisible extra man as he moved about behind my shoulder. Dogs are cheerful companions.

I explained to Strickland, as gently as might be, that I would go over to the Club and find for myself quarters there. I admired his hospitality, was pleased with his guns and rods, but I did not much care for his house and its atmosphere. He heard me out to the end, and then smiled very wearily, but without contempt, for he is a man who understands things. 'Stay on,' he said, 'and see what this thing means. All you have talked about I have known since I took the bungalow. Stay on and wait. Tietjens has left me. Are you going too?'

I had seen him through one little affair, connected with a heathen idol, that had brought me to the doors of a lunatic asylum, and I had no desire to help him through further experiences. He was a man to whom unpleasantnesses arrived as do dinners to ordinary people.

Therefore, I explained more clearly than ever that I liked him immensely, and would be happy to see him in the daytime; but that I did not care to sleep under his roof. This was after dinner, when Tietjens had gone out to lie in the verandah.

"Pon my soul, I don't wonder,' said Strickland, with his eyes on the ceiling cloth. 'Look at that!'

The tails of two brown snakes were hanging between the cloth and the cornice of the wall. They threw long shadows in the lamplight.

'If you are afraid of snakes of course—' said Strickland.

I hate and fear snakes, because if you look into the eyes of any snake you will see that it knows all and more of the mystery of man's fall, and that it feels all the contempt that the Devil felt when Adam was evicted from Eden. Besides which, its bite is generally fatal, and it twists up trouser legs.

'You ought to get your thatch overhauled,' I said.

'Give me a mahseer-rod, and we'll poke 'em down.'

'They'll hide among the roof-beams,' said Strickland. 'I can't stand snakes overhead. I'm going up into the roof. If I shake them down, stand by with a cleaning-rod and break their backs.'

I was not anxious to assist Strickland in his work, but I took the cleaning-rod and waited in the dining room, while Strickland brought a gardener's ladder from the verandah, and set it against the side of the room.

The snake tails drew themselves up and disappeared. We could hear the dry rushing scuttle of long bodies running over the baggy ceiling cloth. Strickland took a lamp with him, while I tried to make clear to him the danger of hunting roof snakes between a ceiling cloth and a thatch, apart from the deterioration of property caused by ripping out ceiling clothes.

'Nonsense!' said Strickland. 'They're sure to hide near the walls by the cloth. The bricks are too cold for 'em, and the heat of the room is just what they like.'

He put his hand to the corner of the stuff and ripped it from the cornice. It gave with a great sound of tearing, and Strickland put his head through the opening into the dark of the angle of the roof beams. I set my teeth and lifted the rod, for I had not the least knowledge of what might descend.

'H'm!' said Strickland, and his voice rolled and rumbled in the roof. 'There's room for another set of rooms up here, and, by Jove, someone is occupying 'em!'

'Snakes?' I said from below.

'No. It's a buffalo. Hand me up the two last joints of a mahseer-rod, and I'll prod it. It's lying on the main roof beam.'

I handed up the rod.

'What a nest for owls and serpents! No wonder the snakes live here,' said Strickland, climbing farther into the roof. I could see his elbow thrusting with the rod. 'Come out of that, whoever you are! Heads below there! It's falling.'

I saw the ceiling cloth nearly in the centre of the room bag with a shape that was pressing it downwards and downwards towards the lighted lamp on the table. I snatched the lamp out of danger and stood back. Then the cloth ripped out from the walls, tore, split, swayed, and shot down upon the table something that I dared not look at, till Strickland had slid down the ladder and was standing by my side.

He did not say much, being a man of few words; but he picked up the loose end of the tablecloth and threw it over the remnants on the table.

'It strikes me,' said he, putting down the lamp, 'our friend Imray has come back. Oh! You would, would you?'

There was a movement under the cloth, and a little snake wriggled out, to be back-broken by the butt of the mahseer-rod. I was sufficiently sick to make no remarks worth recording.

Strickland meditated, and helped himself to drinks. The arrangement under the cloth made no more signs of life.

'Is it Imray?' I said.

Strickland turned back the cloth for a moment, and looked.

'It is Imray,' he said; 'and his throat is cut from ear to ear.'

Then we spoke, both together and to ourselves: 'That's why he whispered about the house.'

Tietjens, in the garden, began to bay furiously. A little later her great nose heaved open the dining room door.

She sniffed and was still. The tattered ceiling cloth hung down almost to the level of the table, and there was hardly room to move away from the discovery.

Tietjens came in and sat down; her teeth bared under her lip and her forepaws planted. She looked at Strickland.

'It's a bad business, old lady,' said he. 'Men don't climb up into the roofs of their bungalows to die, and they don't fasten up the ceiling cloth behind 'em. Let's think it out.'

'Let's think it out somewhere else,' I said.

'Excellent idea! Turn the lamps out. We'll get into my room.'

I did not turn the lamps out. I went into Strickland's room first, and allowed him to make the darkness. Then he followed me, and we lit tobacco and thought. Strickland thought. I smoked furiously because I was afraid.

'Imray is back,' said Strickland. 'The question is—who killed Imray? Don't talk, I've a notion of my own. When I took this bungalow I took over most of Imray's servants. Imray was guileless and inoffensive, wasn't he?'

I agreed; though the heap under the cloth had looked neither one thing nor the other.

'If I call in all the servants they will stand fast in a crowd and lie like Aryans. What do you suggest?'

'Call 'em in one by one,' I said.

'They'll run away and give the news to all their fellows,' said Strickland. 'We must segregate 'em. Do you suppose your servant knows anything about it?'

'He may, for aught I know; but I don't think it's likely. He has only been here two or three days,' I answered. 'What's your notion?'

'I can't quite tell. How the dickens did the man get the wrong side of the ceiling cloth?'

There was a heavy coughing outside Strickland's bedroom door. This showed that Bahadur Khan, his body servant, had waked from sleep and wished to put Strickland to bed.

'Come in,' said Strickland. 'It's a very warm night, isn't it?'

Bahadur Khan, a great, green-turbaned, six foot Mahomedan, said that it was a very warm night; but that there was more rain pending, which, by his Honour's favour, would bring relief to the country.

'It will be so, if God pleases,' said Strickland, tugging off his boots. 'It is in my mind, Bahadur Khan, that I have worked thee remorselessly for many days—ever since that time when thou first entered into my service. What time was that?'

'Has the Heaven-born forgotten? It was when Imray Sahib went secretly to Europe without warning given; and I—even I—came into the honoured service of the protector of the poor.'

'And Imray Sahib went to Europe?'

'It is so said among those who were his servants.'

'And thou wilt take service with him when he returns?'

'Assuredly, Sahib. He was a good master, and cherished his dependants.'

'That is true. I am very tired, but I go buck shooting tomorrow. Give me the little sharp rifle that I use for black buck; it is in the case yonder.'

The man stooped over the case; handed barrels, stock and

fore-end to Strickland, who fitted all together, yawning dolefully. Then he reached down to the gun case, took a solid-drawn cartridge, and slipped it into the breech of the '360 Express.

'And Imray Sahib has gone to Europe secretly! That is very strange, Bahadur Khan, is it not?'

'What do I know of the ways of the white man, Heaven-born?'

'Very little, truly. But thou shalt know more anon. It has reached me that Imray Sahib has returned from his so long journeyings, and that even now he lies in the next room, waiting his servant.'

'Sahib!'

The lamplight slid along the barrels of the rifle as they levelled themselves at Bahadur Khan's broad breast.

'Go and look!' said Strickland. 'Take a lamp. Thy master is tired, and he waits thee. Go!'

The man picked up a lamp, and went into the dining room, Strickland following, and almost pushing him with the muzzle of the rifle. He looked for a moment at the black depths behind the ceiling cloth; at the writhing snake under foot; and last, a grey glaze settling on his face, at the thing under the tablecloth.

'Hast thou seen?' said Strickland after a pause.

'I have seen. I am clay in the white man's hands. What does the Presence do?'

'Hang thee within the month. What else?'

'For killing him? Nay, Sahib, consider. Walking among us, his servants, he cast his eyes upon my child, who was four years old. Him he bewitched, and in ten days he died of the fever—my child!'

'What said Imray Sahib?'

'He said he was a handsome child, and patted him on the head; wherefore my child died. Wherefore, I killed Imray Sahib in the twilight, when he had come back from office, and was sleeping. Wherefore I dragged him up into the roof beams and made all fast behind him. The Heaven-born knows all things. I am the servant of the Heaven-born.'

Strickland looked at me above the rifle, and said, in the vernacular, 'Thou art witness to this saying? He has killed.'

Bahadur Khan stood ashen grey in the light of the one lamp. The need for justification came upon him very swiftly. 'I am trapped,' he said, 'but the offence was that man's. He cast an evil eye upon my child, and I killed and hid him. Only such as are served by devils,' he glared at Tietjens, couched stolidly before him, 'only such could know what I did.'

'It was clever. But thou shouldst have lashed him to the beam with a rope. Now, thou thyself wilt hang by a rope. Orderly!'

A drowsy policeman answered Strickland's call. He was followed by another, and Tietjens sat wondrous still.

'Take him to the police station,' said Strickland. 'There is a case toward.'

'Do I hang, then?' said Bahadur Khan, making no attempt to escape, and keeping his eyes on the ground.

'If the sun shines or the water runs—yes!' said Strickland.

Bahadur Khan stepped back one long pace, quivered and stood still. The two policemen waited further orders.

'Go!' said Strickland.

'Nay; but I go very swiftly,' said Bahadur Khan. 'Look! I am even now a dead man.'

He lifted his foot, and to the little toe there clung the head of the half-killed snake, firm fixed in the agony of death.

'I come of land-holding stock,' said Bahadur Khan, rocking where he stood. 'It were a disgrace to me to go to the public scaffold, therefore I take this way. Be it remembered that the Sahib's shirts are correctly enumerated, and that there is an extra piece of soap in his washbasin. My child was bewitched, and I slew the wizard. Why should you seek to slay me with the rope? My honour is saved, and—and—I die.'

At the end of an hour he died, as they die who are bitten by the little brown karait, and the policemen bore him and the thing under the tablecloth to their appointed places. All were needed to make clear the disappearance of Imray.

'This,' said Strickland, very calmly, as he climbed into bed, 'is called the nineteenth century. Did you hear what that man said?'

'I heard,' I answered. 'Imray made a mistake.'

'Simply and solely through not knowing the nature of the Oriental, and the coincidence of a little seasonal fever. Bahadur Khan had been with him for four years.'

I shuddered. My own servant had been with me for exactly that length of time. When I went over to my own room I found my man waiting, impassive as the copper head on a penny, to pull off my boots.

'What has befallen Bahadur Khan?' said I.

'He was bitten by a snake and died. The rest the Sahib knows,' was the answer.

'And how much of this matter hast thou known?'

'As much as might be gathered from one coming in in the twilight to seek satisfaction. Gently, Sahib. Let me pull off those boots.'

I had just settled to the sleep of exhaustion when I heard Strickland shouting from his side of the house—

"Tietjens has come back to her place!'

And so she had. The great deerhound was couched statelily on her own bedstead on her own blanket, while, in the next room, the idle, empty, ceiling cloth waggled as it trailed on the table.

THE EMPTY HOUSE

Algernon Blackwood

Certain houses, like certain persons, manage somehow to proclaim at once their character for evil. In the case of the latter, no particular feature need betray them; they may boast an open countenance and an ingenuous smile; and yet a little of their company leaves the unalterable conviction that there is something radically amiss with their being: that they are evil. Willy nilly, they seem to communicate an atmosphere of secret and wicked thoughts which makes those in their immediate neighbourhood shrink from them as from a thing diseased.

And, perhaps, with houses the same principle is operative, and it is the aroma of evil deeds committed under a particular roof, long after the actual doers have passed away, that makes the gooseflesh come and the hair rise. Something of the original passion of the evil-doer, and of the horror felt by his victim, enters the heart of the innocent watcher, and he becomes suddenly conscious of tingling nerves, creeping skin, and a chilling of the blood. He is terror-stricken without apparent cause.

There was manifestly nothing in the external appearance of this particular house to bear out the tales of the horror that was said to reign within. It was neither lonely nor unkempt. It stood, crowded into a corner of the square, and looked exactly like the houses on either side of it. It had the same number of windows as its neighbours; the same balcony overlooking the gardens; the same white steps leading up to the heavy black front door; and, in the rear, there was the same narrow strip of green, with neat box borders, running up to the wall that divided it from the backs of the adjoining houses. Apparently, too, the number of chimney pots on the roof was the same; the breadth and angle of the eaves; and even the height of the dirty area railings.

And yet this house in the square, that seemed precisely similar to its fifty ugly neighbours, was, as a matter of fact, entirely different—horribly different.

Wherein lay this marked, invisible difference is impossible to say. It cannot be ascribed wholly to the imagination, because persons who had spent some time in the house, knowing nothing of the facts, had declared positively that certain rooms were so disagreeable they would rather die than enter them again, and that the atmosphere of the whole house produced in them symptoms of a genuine terror; while the series of innocent tenants who had tried to live in it and been forced to decamp at the shortest possible notice, was indeed little less than a scandal in the town.

When Shorthouse arrived to pay a 'weekend' visit to his Aunt Julia in her little house on the seafront at the other end of the town, he found her charged to the brim with mystery and excitement. He had only received her telegram that morning, and he had come anticipating boredom; but the moment he touched her hand and kissed her apple-skin wrinkled cheek, he caught the first waves of her electrical condition. The impression deepened when he learned that there were to be no other visitors, and that he had been telegraphed for with a very special object.

Something was in the wind, and the 'something' would doubtless bear fruit; for this elderly spinster aunt, with a mania for psychical research, had brains as well as willpower, and by hook or by crook, she usually managed to accomplish her ends. The revelation was made soon after tea, when she sidled close up to him as they paced slowly along the seafront in the dusk.

'I've got the keys,' she announced in a delighted, yet half awesome voice. 'Got them till Monday!'

'The keys of the bathing-machine, or—?' he asked innocently; looking from the sea to the town. Nothing brought her so quickly to the point as feigning stupidity.

'Neither,' she whispered. 'I've got the keys of the haunted house in the square—and I'm going there tonight.'

Shorthouse was conscious of the slightest possible tremor down his back. He dropped his teasing tone. Something in her voice and manner thrilled him. She was in earnest.

'But you can't go alone—' he began.

'That's why I wired for you,' she said with decision.

He turned to look at her. The ugly, lined, enigmatical face was alive with excitement. There was the glow of genuine enthusiasm round it like a halo. The eyes shone. He caught another wave of her excitement, and a second tremor, more marked than the first, accompanied it.

'Thanks, Aunt Julia,' he said politely; 'thanks awfully.'

'I should not dare to go quite alone,' she went on, raising her voice; 'But with you I should enjoy it immensely. You're afraid of nothing, I know.'

'Thanks so much,' he said again. 'Er—is anything likely to happen?'

'A great deal *has* happened,' she whispered, 'though it's been most cleverly hushed up. Three tenants have come and gone in the last few months, and the house is said to be empty for good now.'

In spite of himself, Shorthouse became interested. His aunt was so very much in earnest.

'The house is very old indeed,' she went on, 'and the story—an unpleasant one—dates a long way back. It has to do with a murder committed by a jealous stableman who had some affair with a servant in the house. One night he managed to secrete himself in the cellar, and when everyone was asleep, he crept upstairs to the servants' quarters, chased the girl down to the next landing, and before anyone could come to the rescue threw her bodily over the bannisters into the hall below.'

'And the stableman—?'

'Was caught, I believe, and hanged for murder; but it all happened a century ago, and I've not been able to get more details of the story.'

Shorthouse now felt his interest thoroughly aroused but, though he was not particularly nervous for himself, he hesitated a little on his aunt's account.

'On one condition,' he said at length.

'Nothing will prevent my going,' she said firmly; 'but I may as well hear your condition.'

'That you guarantee your power of self-control if anything really horrible happens. I mean—that you are sure you won't get too frightened.'

'Jim,' she said scornfully, 'I'm not young, I know, nor are my nerves; but *with you* I should be afraid of nothing in the world!'

This, of course, settled it, for Shorthouse had no pretensions to being other than a very ordinary young man, and an appeal to his vanity was irresistible. He agreed to go.

Instinctively; by a sort of subconscious preparation, he kept himself and his forces well in hand the whole evening, compelling an accumulative reserve of control by that nameless inward process of gradually putting all the emotions away and turning the key upon them—a process difficult to describe, but wonderfully effective, as all men who have lived through severe trials of the inner man well understand. Later, it stood him in good stead.

But it was not until half past ten, when they stood in the hall, well in the glare of friendly lamps and still surrounded by comforting human influences, that he had to make the first call upon this store of collected strength. For, once the door was closed, and he saw the deserted silent street stretching away white in the moonlight before them, it came to him clearly that the real test that night would be in dealing with *two fears* instead of one. He would have to carry his aunt's fear as well as his own. And, as he glanced down at her sphinx-like countenance and realized that it might assume no pleasant aspect in a rush of real terror, he felt satisfied with only one thing in the whole adventure—that he had confidence in his own will and power to stand against any shock that might come.

Slowly they walked along the empty streets of the town; a bright autumn moon silvered the roofs, casting deep shadows; there was no breath of wind; and the trees in the formal gardens by the seafront watched them silently as they passed along. To his aunt's occasional remarks Shorthouse made no reply; realizing that she was simply surrounding herself with mental buffers—saying ordinary things to prevent herself thinking of extraordinary things. Few windows showed lights, and from scarcely a single chimney came smoke or sparks. Shorthouse had already begun to notice everything, even the smallest details. Presently, they stopped at the street corner and looked up at the name on the side of the house full in the moonlight, and with one accord, but without remark, turned into the square and crossed over to the side of it that lay in shadow.

'The number of the house is thirteen,' whispered a voice at his side; and neither of them made the obvious reference, but passed across the broad sheet of moonlight and began to march up the pavement in silence.

It was about halfway up the square that Shorthouse felt an arm slip quietly but significantly into his own, and knew then that their adventure had begun in earnest, and that his companion was already yielding imperceptibly to the influences against them. She needed support.

A few minutes later they stopped before a tall, narrow house that rose before them into the night, ugly in shape and painted a dingy white. Shutterless windows, without blinds, stared down upon them, shining here and there in the moonlight. There were weather streaks in the wall and cracks in the paint, and the balcony bulged out from the first floor a little unnaturally. But, beyond this generally forlorn appearance of an unoccupied house, there was nothing at first sight to single out this particular mansion for the evil character it had most certainly acquired.

Taking a look over their shoulders to make sure they had not been followed, they went boldly up the steps and stood against the huge black door that fronted them forbiddingly. But the first wave of nervousness was now upon them, and Shorthouse fumbled a long time with the key before he could fit it into the lock at all. For a moment, if truth were told, they both hoped it would not open, for they were a prey to various unpleasant emotions as they stood there on the threshold of their ghostly adventure. Shorthouse, shuffling with the key and hampered by the steady weight on his arm, certainly felt the solemnity of the moment. It was as if the whole world—for all experience seemed at that instant concentrated in his own consciousness—were listening to the grating noise of that key.

A stray puff of wind wandering down the empty street woke a momentary rustling in the trees behind them, but otherwise this rattling of the key was the only sound audible; and at last it turned in the lock and the heavy door swung open and revealed a yawning gulf of darkness beyond.

With a last glance at the moonlit square, they passed quickly in, and the door slammed behind them with a roar that echoed prodigiously through empty halls and passages. But, instantly, with the echoes, another sound made itself heard, and Aunt Julia leaned suddenly so heavily upon him that he had to take a step backwards to save himself from falling.

A man had coughed close beside them—so close that it seemed they must have been actually by his side in the darkness.

With the possibility of practical jokes in his mind, Shorthouse at once swung his heavy stick in the direction of the sound; but it met nothing more solid than air. He heard his aunt give a little gasp beside him.

'There's someone here,' she whispered. 'I heard him.'

'Be quiet!' he said sternly. 'It was nothing but the noise of the front door.'

'Oh! Get a light—quick!' she added, as her nephew fumbling with a box of matches, opened it upside down and let them all fall with a rattle on to the stone floor.

The sound, however, was not repeated; and there was no evidence of retreating footsteps. In another minute they had a candle burning, using an empty end of a cigar case as a holder; and when the first flare had died down he held the impromptu lamp aloft and surveyed the scene. And it was dreary enough in all conscience, for there is nothing more desolate in all the abodes of men than an unfurnished house, dimly lit, silent and forsaken, and yet tenanted by rumour with the memories of evil and violent histories.

They were standing in a wide hallway; on their left was the open door of a spacious dining room, and in front the hall ran, ever narrowing, into a long, dark passage that led apparently to the top of the kitchen stairs. The broad uncarpeted staircase rose in a sweep before them, everywhere draped in shadows, except for a single spot about halfway up where the moonlight came in through the window and fell on a bright patch on the boards. This shaft of light shed a faint radiance above and below it, lending to the objects within its reach a misty outline that was infinitely more suggestive and ghostly than complete darkness. Filtered moonlight always seems to paint faces on the surrounding gloom, and as Shorthouse peered up into the well of darkness and thought of the countless empty rooms and passages in the upper part of the old house, he caught himself longing again for the safety of the moonlit square, or the cosy, bright drawing room they had left an hour before. Then realizing that these thoughts were dangerous, he thrust them away again and summoned all his energy for concentration on the present.

'Aunt Julia,' he said aloud, severer; 'we must now go through the house from top to bottom and make a thorough search.'

The echoes of his voice died away slowly all over the building, and in the intense silence that followed he turned to look at her. In the candlelight he saw that her face was already ghastly pale; but she dropped his arm for a moment and said in a whisper, stepping close in front of him—

'I agree. We must be sure there's no one hiding. That's the first thing.'

She spoke with evident effort, and he looked at her with admiration.

'You feel quite sure of yourself? It's not too late—'

'I think so,' she whispered, her eyes shifting nervously toward the shadows behind. 'Quite sure, only one thing—'

'What's that?'

'You must never leave me alone for an instant.'

'As long as you understand that any sound or appearance must be investigated at once, for to hesitate means to admit fear. That is fatal.'

'Agreed,' she said, a little shakily; after a moment's hesitation. 'I'll try—'

Arm in arm, Shorthouse holding the dripping candle and the stick, while his aunt carried the cloak over her shoulders, figures of utter comedy to all but themselves, they began a systematic search. Stealthily, walking on tiptoe and shading the candle lest it should betray their presence through the shutterless windows, they went first into the big dining room. There was not a stick of furniture to be seen. Bare walls, ugly mantelpieces and empty grates stared at them. Everything, they felt, resented their intrusion, watching them, as it were, with veiled eyes; whispers followed them; shadows flitted noiselessly to right and left; something seemed ever at their back, watching, waiting an opportunity to do them injury. There was the inevitable sense that operations which went on when the room was empty had been temporarily suspended till they were well out of the way again. The whole dark interior of the old building seemed to become a malignant Presence that rose up, warning them to desist and mind their own business; every moment the strain on the nerves increased.

Out of the gloomy dining room they passed through large folding doors into a sort of library or smoking room, wrapt equally in silence, darkness and dust; and from this they regained the hall near the top of the back stairs.

Here a pitch black tunnel opened before them into the lower regions, and—it must be confessed—they hesitated. But only for a minute. With the worst of the night still to come, it was essential to turn from nothing. Aunt Julia stumbled at the top step of the dark descent, ill-lit by the flickering candle, and even Shorthouse felt at least half the decision go out of his legs.

'Come on!' he said peremptorily, and his voice ran on and lost itself in the dark, empty spaces below.

'I'm coming,' she faltered, catching his arm with unnecessary violence.

They went a little unsteadily down the stone steps, a cold, damp air meeting them in the face, close and malodorous. The kitchen, into which the stairs led along a narrow passage, was large, with a lofty ceiling. Several doors opened out of it—some into cupboards with empty jars still standing on the shelves, and others into horrible little ghostly back offices, each colder and less inviting than the last. Black beetles scurried over the floor, and once, when they knocked against a deal table standing in a corner, something about the size of a cat jumped down with a rush and fled, scampering across the stone floor into the darkness. Everywhere there was a sense of recent occupation, an impression of sadness and gloom.

Leaving the plain kitchen, they next went towards the scullery. The door was standing ajar, and as they pushed it open to its full extent Aunt Julia uttered a piercing scream, which she instantly tried to stifle by placing her hand over her mouth. For a second Shorthouse stood stock-still, catching his breath. He felt as if his spine had suddenly become hollow and someone had filled it with particles of ice.

Facing them, directly in their way between the doorposts, stood the figure of a woman. She had dishevelled hair and wildly staring eyes, and her face was terrified and white as death.

She stood there motionless for the space of a single second. Then the candle flickered and she was gone—gone utterly—and the door framed nothing but empty darkness.

'Only the beastly jumping candlelight,' he said quickly, in a voice that sounded like someone else's and was only half under control. 'Come on, aunt. There's nothing there.'

He dragged her forward. With a clattering of feet and a great appearance of boldness they went on, but over his body the skin moved as if crawling ants covered it, and he knew by the weight on his arm that he was supplying the force of locomotion for two. The scullery was cold, bare and empty; more like a large prison cell than anything else. They went round it, tried the door into the yard, and the windows, but found them all fastened securely. His aunt moved beside him like a person in a dream. Her eyes were tightly shut, and she seemed merely to follow the pressure of his arm. Her courage filled him with amazement. At the same time he noticed that a certain odd change had come over her face, a change which somehow evaded his power of analysis.

'There's nothing here, aunty,' he repeated aloud quickly, 'Let's go upstairs and see the rest of the house. Then we'll choose a room to wait up in.'

She followed him obediently keeping close to his side, and they locked the kitchen door behind them. It was a relief to get up again. In the hall there was more light than before, for the moon had travelled a little further down the stairs. Cautiously they began to go up into the dark vault of the upper house, the boards creaking under their weight.

On the first floor they found the large double drawing rooms, a search of which revealed nothing. Here also was no sign of furniture or recent occupancy; nothing but dust and neglect and shadows. They opened the big folding doors between front and back drawing rooms and then came out again to the landing and went on upstairs.

They had not gone up more than a dozen steps when they

both simultaneously stopped to listen, looking into each other's eyes with a new apprehension across the flickering candle flame. From the room they had left hardly ten seconds before came the sound of doors quietly closing. It was beyond all question; they heard the booming noise that accompanies the shutting of heavy doors, followed by the sharp catching of the latch.

'We must go back and see,' said Shorthouse briefly, in a low tone, and turning to go downstairs again.

Somehow she managed to drag after him, her feet catching in her dress, her face livid.

When they entered the front drawing room, it was plain that the folding doors had been closed—half a minute before. Without hesitation Shorthouse opened them. He almost expected to see someone facing him in the back room; but only darkness and cold air met him. They went through both rooms, finding nothing unusual. They tried in every way to make the doors close of themselves, but there was not wind enough even to set the candle flame flickering. The doors would not move without strong pressure. All was silent as the grave. Undeniably the rooms were utterly empty; and the house utterly still.

'It's beginning,' whispered a voice at his elbow which he hardly recognized as his aunt's.

He nodded acquiescence, taking out his watch to note the time. It was fifteen minutes before midnight; he made the entry of exactly what had occurred in his notebook, setting the candle in its case upon the floor in order to do so. It took a moment or two to balance it safely against the wall.

Aunt Julia always declared that at this moment she was not actually watching him, but had turned her head towards the inner room, where she fancied she heard something moving; but, at any rate, both positively agreed that there came a sound of rushing feet, heavy and very swift—and the next instant the candle was out!

But to Shorthouse himself had come more than this, and he has always thanked his fortunate stars that it came to him alone and not to his aunt too. For, as he rose from the stooping position of balancing the candle, and before it was actually extinguished, a face thrust itself forward so close to his own that he could almost have touched it with his lips. It was a face working with passion—a man's face, dark, with thick features and angry, savage eyes. It belonged to a common man, and it was evil in its ordinary normal expression, no doubt, but as he saw it, alive with intense, aggressive emotion it was a malignant and terrible human countenance.

There was no movement of the air; nothing but the sound of rushing feet—stockinged or muffled feet; the apparition of the face; and the almost simultaneous extinguishing of the candle.

In spite of himself, Shorthouse uttered a little cry, nearly losing his balance as his aunt clung to him with her whole weight in one moment of real, uncontrollable terror. She made no sound, but simply seized him bodily. Fortunately, however, she had seen nothing, but had only heard the rushing feet, for her control returned almost at once, and he was able to disentangle himself and strike a match.

The shadows ran away on all sides before the glare, and his aunt stooped down and groped for the cigar case with the precious candle. Then they discovered that the candle had not been blown out at all; it had been *crushed* out. The wick was pressed down into the wax, which was flattened as if by some smooth, heavy instrument.

How his companion so quickly overcame her terror, Shorthouse never properly understood; but his admiration for her self-control increased tenfold, and at the same time served to feed his own dying flame—for which he was undeniably grateful. Equally inexplicable to him was the evidence of physical force they had just witnessed. He at once suppressed the memory of stories he had heard of 'physical mediums' and their dangerous phenomena; for if these were true, and either his aunt or himself was unwittingly a physical medium, it meant that they were simply aiding to focus the forces of a haunted house already charged to the brim. It was like walking with unprotected lamps among uncovered stores of gunpowder.

So, with as little reflection as possible, he simply relit the candle and went up to the next floor. The arm in his trembled, it is true, and his own tread was often uncertain, but they went on with thoroughness, and after a search revealing nothing, they climbed the last flight of stairs to the top floor of all.

Here they found a perfect nest of small servants' rooms, with broken pieces of furniture, dirty cane-bottomed chairs, chests of drawers, cracked mirrors and decrepit bedsteads. The rooms had low sloping ceilings already hung here and there with cobwebs, small windows, and badly plastered walls—a depressing and dismal region which they were glad to leave behind.

It was on the stroke of midnight when they entered a small room on the third floor, close to the top of the stairs, and arranged to make themselves comfortable for the remainder of their adventure. It was absolutely bare, and was said to be the room—then used as a clothes closet—into which the infuriated groom had chased his victim and finally caught her. Outside, across the narrow landing, began the stairs leading up to the floor above, and the servants' quarters where they had just searched.

In spite of the chilliness of the night there was something in the air of this room that cried for an open window. But there was more than this. Shorthouse could only describe it by saying that he felt less master of himself here than in any other part of the house. There was something that acted directly on the nerves, tiring the resolution, enfeebling the will. He was conscious of this result before he had been in the room five minutes, and it was in the short time they stayed there that he suffered the wholesale depletion of his vital forces, which was, for himself, the chief horror of the whole experience.

They put the candle on the floor of the cupboard, leaving the door a few inches ajar, so that there was no glare to confuse the eyes, and no shadow to shift about on walls and ceiling. Then they spread the cloak on the floor and sat down to wait, with their backs against the wall.

Shorthouse was within two feet of the door on to the landing; his position commanded a good view of the main staircase leading down into the darkness, and also of the beginning of the servants' stairs going to the floor above; the heavy stick lay beside him within easy reach.

The moon was now high above the house. Through the open window, they could see the comforting stars like friendly eyes watching in the sky. One by one the clocks of the town struck midnight, and when the sounds died away the deep silence of a windless night fell again over everything. Only the boom of the sea, far away and lugubrious, filled the air with hollow murmurs.

Inside the house the silence became awful; awful, he thought, because any minute now it might be broken by sounds portending terror. The strain of waiting told more and more severely on the nerves; they talked in whispers when they talked at all, for their voices aloud sounded queer and unnatural. A chilliness, not altogether due to the night air, invaded the room, and made them cold. The influences against them, whatever these might be, were slowly robbing them of self-confidence, and the power of decisive action: their forces were on the wane, and the possibility of real fear took on a new and terrible meaning. He began to tremble for the elderly woman by his side, whose pluck could hardly save her beyond a certain extent.

He heard the blood singing in his veins. It sometimes seemed so loud that he fancied it prevented his hearing properly certain other sounds that were beginning very faintly to make themselves audible in the depths of the house. Every time he fastened his attention on these sounds, they instantly ceased. They certainly came no nearer. Yet he could not rid himself of the idea that movement was going on somewhere in the lower regions of the house. The drawing rooms' floor, where the door had been so strangely closed, seemed too near; the sounds were further off than that. He thought of the great kitchen, with the scurrying black beetles, and of the dismal little scullery; but, somehow or other, they did not seem to come from there either. Surely they were not *outside* the house!

Then, suddenly, the truth flashed into his mind, and for the space of a minute he felt as if his blood had stopped flowing and turned to ice.

The sounds were not downstairs at all; they were *upstairs*—upstairs, somewhere among those horrid gloomy little servants' rooms with their bits of broken furniture, low ceilings, and cramped windows—upstairs where the victim had first been disturbed and stalked to her death.

And the moment he discovered where the sounds were, he began to hear them more clearly. It was the sound of feet, moving stealthily along the passage overhead, in and out among the rooms, and past the furniture.

He turned quickly to steal a glance at the motionless figure seated beside him, to note whether she had shared his discovery. The faint candlelight coming through the crack in the cupboard door, threw her strongly-marked face into vivid relief against the white of the wall. But it was something else that made him catch his breath and stare again. An extraordinary something had come into her face and seemed to spread over her features like a mask; it smoothed out the deep lines and drew the skin everywhere a little tighter so that the wrinkles disappeared; it brought into the face—with the sole exception of the old eyes—an appearance of youth and almost of childhood.

He stared in speechless amazement—amazement that was dangerously near to horror. It was his aunt's face indeed, but it was her face of forty years ago, the vacant innocent face of a girl. He had heard stories of that strange effect of terror which could wipe a human countenance clean of other emotions, obliterating all previous expression; but he had never realized that it could be literally true, or could mean anything so simply horrible as what he now saw for the dreadful signature of overmastering fear was written plainly in that utter vacancy of the girlish face beside him; and when, feeling his intense gaze, she turned to look at him, he instinctively closed his eyes tightly to shut out the sight.

Yet, when he turned a minute later, his feelings well in hand, he saw to his intense relief another expression; his aunt was smiling, and though the face was deathly white, the awful veil had lifted and the normal look was returning.

'Anything wrong?' was all he could think of to say at the moment. And the answer was eloquent, coming from such a woman.

'I feel cold—and a little frightened,' she whispered.

He offered to close the window, but she seized hold of him and begged him not to leave her side even for an instant.

'It's upstairs, I know,' she whispered, with an odd half laugh; 'but I can't possibly go up.'

But Shorthouse thought otherwise, knowing that in action lay their best hope of self-control.

He took the brandy flask and poured out a glass of neat spirit, stiff enough to help anybody over anything. She swallowed it with a little shiver. His only idea now was to get out of the house before her collapse became inevitable; but this could not safely be done by turning tail and running from the enemy. Inaction was no longer possible; every minute, he was growing less master of himself, and desperate, aggressive measures were imperative without further delay. Moreover, the action must be taken *towards* the enemy; not away from it; the climax, if necessary and unavoidable, would have to be faced boldly. He could do it now; but in ten minutes he might not have the force left to act for himself, much less for both!

Upstairs, the sounds were meanwhile becoming louder and closer, accompanied by occasional creaking of the boards. Someone was moving stealthily about, stumbling now and then awkwardly against the furniture.

Waiting a few moments to allow the tremendous dose of spirits to produce its effect, and knowing this would last but a short time under the circumstances, Shorthouse then quietly got on his feet, saying in a determined voice—

'Now, Aunt Julia, we'll go upstairs and find out what all this noise is about. You must come too. It's what we agreed.'

He picked up his stick and went to the cupboard for the candle. A limp form rose shakily beside him breathing hard, and he heard a voice say very faintly something about being 'ready to come'. The woman's courage amazed him; it was so much greater than his own and, as they advanced, holding aloft the dripping candle, some subtle force exhaled from this trembling, white-faced old woman at his side that was the true source of his inspiration. It held something really great that shamed him and gave him the support without which he would have proved far less equal to the occasion.

They crossed the dark landing, avoiding with their eyes the deep black space over the banisters. Then they began to mount the narrow staircase to meet the sounds which, minute by minute, grew louder and nearer. About halfway up the stairs Aunt Julia stumbled and Shorthouse turned to catch her by the arm, and just at that moment there came a terrific crash in the servants' corridor overhead. It was instantly followed by a shrill, agonized scream that was a cry of terror and a cry for help melted into one.

Before they could move aside, or go down a single step, someone came rushing along the passage overhead, blundering horribly, racing madly, at full speed, three steps at a time, down the very staircase where they stood. The steps were light and uncertain; but close behind them sounded the heavier tread of another person, and the staircase seemed to shake.

Shorthouse and his companion just had time to flatten themselves against the wall when the jumble of flying steps was upon them, and two persons, with the slightest possible interval between them, dashed past at full speed. It was a perfect whirlwind of sound breaking in upon the midnight silence of the empty building.

The two runners, pursuer and pursued, had passed clean through them where they stood, and already with a thud the boards below had received first one, then the other. Yet they had seen absolutely nothing—not a hand, or arm, or face, or even a shred of flying clothing.

There came a second's pause. Then the first one, the lighter of the two, obviously the pursued one, ran with uncertain footsteps into the little room which Shorthouse and his aunt had just left. The heavier one followed. There was a sound of scuffling, gasping, and smothered screaming; and then out on to the landing came the step—of a single person *treading weightily*.

A dead silence followed for the space of half a minute, and then was heard a rushing sound through the air. It was followed by a dull, crashing thud in the depths of the house below—on the stone floor of the hall.

Utter silence reigned after. Nothing moved. The flame of the candle was steady. It had been steady the whole time, and the air had been undisturbed by any movement whatsoever. Palsied with terror, Aunt Julia, without waiting for her companion, began fumbling her way downstairs; she was crying gently to herself, and when Shorthouse put his arm round her and half carried her, he felt that she was trembling like a leaf. He went into the little room and picked up the cloak from the floor, and, arm in arm, walking very slowly, without speaking a word or looking once behind them, they marched down the three flights into the hall.

In the hall they saw nothing, but the whole way down the stairs they were conscious that someone followed them; step by step; when they went faster IT was left behind, and when they went more slowly IT caught them up. But never once did they look behind to see; and at each turning of the staircase they lowered their eyes for fear of the following horror they might see upon the stairs above.

With trembling hands Shorthouse opened the front door, and they walked out into the moonlight and drew a deep breath of the cool night air blowing in from the sea.

CHUNIA, AYAH

Alice Perrin

'I hope you clearly understand that I do not believe in ghosts?'

The little grey-haired spinster paused and regarded me with suspicion, and alarmed lest I should, after all, lose the story I had been so carefully stalking, I vehemently reassured her on the point, whereupon, to my relief, she continued—

'It certainly was a most extraordinary thing, and even now I hardly know what to make of it, though it happened a long time ago. One cold weather when I was in India keeping house for my brother, I received a letter from a friend, begging me to pay her a long promised visit. She wrote that her husband was going into camp for a month to a part of his district where she could not accompany him, so that she and her little girl would be all alone, and I should be doing her a great kindness by coming. So the end of it was I accepted the invitation, though I greatly disliked leaving my brother to the tender mercies of the servants, and after a long, hot journey arrived at my destination at five o'clock one evening.

'My friend, Mrs Pollock, was on the platform to meet me, and outside the station a bamboo cart was waiting, into which we climbed, and were soon bowling along the hard, white road at a brisk pace. Mary at once began to relate anecdotes of her little girl, whose name was Dot—how tall she was for her age (twenty months!), how much she ate, what she tried to say, what the ayah said about her, and so on.

'Now I must confess that I am not very fond of children; I like them well enough in their proper place (if that is not too near me), but I do not know how to behave towards them, and am always nervous as to what they will do or say next. Therefore, fond as I was of Mary herself, the subject of her conversation did not particularly interest me. When we arrived at the house, she actually inquired which I would do first—see Dot or have some tea! I boldly elected for tea, as I was exceedingly tired and thirsty, and I also reflected that if I did not at once make a determined stand, I should be Dot-ridden" for the remainder of my visit.

'After tea I was taken to my room, and Mary brought her treasure to me for exhibition. She was the most lovely child I had ever beheld, with a grave, sweet face that quite won my unmotherly heart, and for once my prejudices completely melted away. Mary put her into my arms and stood by in an ecstacy of pride and delight as I proceeded to tap the pin-cushion, rattle my keys and perform various idiotic antics in my efforts to amuse Dot, who, I felt sure, would set up a howl in a few moments. But she watched my foolish attempts to be entertaining with an attentive gravity that was quite embarrassing, and charmed though I was with the little creature, I felt relieved when she held out her arms to go back to her mother.

'Mary called for the ayah to come and take the child to her nursery, and a woman with a sullen, handsome face entered and took her charge away. I remarked that the ayah looked bad-tempered, upon which Mary assured me that she could trust the child anywhere with her, and that she was a perfect treasure.

'The next morning I was awakened by a soft little pat on my face, and, opening my eyes, I found Dot holding herself upright by the corner, of my pillow.

'"Why, little one, are you all alone?" I said, lifting her on to the bed, and then I discovered that her feet were wringing wet.

'She held up one wet little foot and examined it carefully, and then pointed to the bathroom door, which was open, and from where I lay I could see an overturned jug and streams of water on the floor—evidently Dot's handiwork. I put on my dressing gown and took the child to her mother, explaining what had happened, and Mary hastily pulled off the soaking little shoes and socks and called for the ayah, who presently entered, and stood silently watching her mistress.

'"What do you mean by leaving the child in this way?" exclaimed Mary, angrily, and gathering up Dot's shoes and socks, she threw them to the ayah, bidding her bring others that were dry. One of the little shoes struck the woman on the cheek, for Mary was annoyed and had flung them with unnecessary force, and never shall I forget the look on the ayah's face as she left the room to carry out the order. It was the face of a devil, but Mary did not see it, for she was busy rubbing the cold little feet in her hands.

'"Mary," I said impulsively, "I am sure the ayah is a brute. Do get rid of her. I never saw anything so dreadful as the look she gave you just now."

'"My dear," answered Mary, with good-humoured impatience, "you have taken an unreasonable dislike to Chunia. She knew she was in the wrong and felt ashamed of herself."

'So the matter dropped; but I could not get over my dislike to Chunia, and as my visit wore on, and I became more and more attached to dear little Dot, I could hardly endure to see the child in her presence.

'My month with Mary passed quickly away, and I was really sorry when it was over, more especially as on my return home, my brother was called away unexpectedly on business, and I was left alone. I missed Dot more than I could have believed possible, for I had become ridiculously devoted to the small, round bundle of humanity, with the great dark eyes and short yellow curls, and my feelings are not to be described when the letter came from Mr Pollock giving me the awful news of the child's death.

'I read the letter over and over again, hardly able to believe it. The whole thing was so hideously sudden! I had only left Mary and Dot such a short time ago, and when last I had seen the child she was in her mother's arms on the platform of the railway station, kissing her little fat hands laboriously to me in farewell, and looking the picture of life and health.

'Poor Mr Pollock wrote in a heartbroken strain. It appeared that the child had strayed away one afternoon and must have fallen into the river, which ran past the bottom of the garden, for the little sun hat was found floating in the stream, and close to the water's edge lay a toy that she had been playing with all day. Every search had been made, but no further trace could be found. The poor mother was distracted with sorrow, and Mr Pollock had telegraphed for leave, as he meant to take her to England at once. He added that the ayah, Chunia, had been absent on three days leave when the dreadful accident happened, or, they both felt convinced, it would never have occurred at all. Mary, he wrote, sent me a message to beg me to take the woman into my service, as she could not endure the idea of one who had been so much with their darling going to strangers, for the poor woman had been a faithful servant, and was stricken and dumb with grief.

'I telegraphed at once that I would take Chunia willingly.

I forgot my old antipathy to her, and only remembered that I should have someone about me who had known and loved the child so well. When the woman arrived I was quite shocked at her altered appearance. Her face seemed to have shrunk to half its former size, and her eyes looked enormous, and shone with a strange brilliancy. She was very quiet at first but burst into a flood of tears when I tried to speak to her of poor little Dot, so I gave it up, as I saw she could hardly bear the subject mentioned.

'She helped me to undress the first night, and then, instead of leaving the room, she stood looking at me without speaking.

'"What is it?" I inquired.

'"Memsahib," she said in a whisper, glancing over her shoulder, "may I sleep in your dressing room tonight?"

'I willingly gave her permission, for I saw that the woman's nerves were unstrung and that she needed companionship. Then I got into bed, and must have been asleep for some hours when I awoke thinking I had heard a shrill voice crying in the compound. I listened, and again it came, a high, beseeching wail. It was certainly the voice of a child, and the awful pleading and despair expressed in the sound was heart-rending. I felt sure some native baby had wandered into the grounds and was calling hopelessly for its mother.

'I lit a candle and went into my dressing room, where to my astonishment, I saw Chunia crouching against the outer door that led into the verandah, holding it fast with both hands as though she were shutting someone out.

'I asked what she was doing, and whether she knew whose child was crying outside. She sprang to her feet and answered sullenly that she had heard no child crying. I opened the door and went out into the verandah, but nothing was to be seen or heard, and I had no reply to my shouts of inquiry; so, concluding that it must have been my fancy, or perhaps some prowling animal, I returned to bed, and slept soundly for the rest of the night.

'The next evening I dined out, and on my return was surprised to hear someone talking in my dressing room. I hurried in, and again found Chunia kneeling in front of the outer door imploring somebody to "go away" at the top of her voice. Directly, when she saw me she came towards me excitedly.

"'Oh! Memsahib!" she shrieked, "tell her to go away!"

"'Tell who?" I demanded.

"'Dottie-baba," she wailed, wringing her hands. "She cries to come to me—listen to her—listen!"

'She held her breath and waited, and I solemnly declare that as I stood and listened with her, I heard a child crying and moaning on the other side of the door. I was mute with horror and bewilderment, while the plaintive cry rose and fell, and then flinging the door open, I held the candle high above my head. There was no need of a light, for the moon was full, but no child could I see, and the verandah was quite empty. I determined to sift the matter to the bottom, so I went to the servants' quarters and called them all up. But no one could account for the crying of a child, and though the compound was thoroughly searched nothing was discovered. So the servants returned to their houses and I to my verandah, where I found Chunia in a most excited state.

"'Memsahib," she said, with her fists clenched and her eyes starting out of her head, "will she go away if I tell you all about it?"

"'Yes, yes," I cried soothingly, "tell me what you like."

"She silently took my wrist and dragged me into the dressing room, shutting the door with the utmost caution.

"'Stand with your back against it," she whispered, "so that she cannot enter."

'I feared I was in the presence of a mad woman, so I did as she bade me, and waited quietly for her story. She walked up and down the room and began to speak in a kind of chant.

'"I did it," she sang. "I killed the child, little Dottie-baba, and she has followed me always. You heard her cry tonight and last night. The memsahib angered me the day she struck me with the shoe, and then a devil entered into my heart. I asked for leave, and went away, but it was too strong, it drew me back, and it said kill! Kill! I fought and struggled against the voice, but it was useless. So on the second day of my leave I crept back and hid among the bushes till I saw the child alone, and then I took her away and killed her. She was so glad to see me, and laughed and talked, but when she saw the devil in my eyes she grew frightened, and cried just as you heard her cry tonight. I took her little white neck in my hands—see memsahib, how large and strong my hands are—and I pressed and pressed until the child was dead, and then the devil left me. I looked and saw what I had done. I could not unclasp her fingers from my skirt, they clung so tightly, so I took it off and wrapped her in it—"

'The woman stopped suddenly. I had listened in silence, repressing the exclamations of horror that rose to my lips.

'"What did you do then?" I asked. Chunia looked wildly round.

'"I forget," she murmured; "the river, I ran quickly to the river—"

'Then there came a shriek from the dry, parched lips, and then flinging her arms above her head she fell at my feet unconscious and foaming at the mouth.

'Afterwards Chunia was found to be raving mad, and the doctor expressed his opinion that she must have been in a more or less dangerous state for some months past. I told him of her terrible confession to me, but he said that possibly the whole thing was a delusion on her part.

'I went to see her once after she had been placed under restraint, but the sight was so saddening that I never went again. She was seated on the floor of her prison patting an imaginary baby to sleep, croning the quaint little lullaby that ayahs always use, and when I spoke to her she only gazed at me with dull, vacant eyes, and continued the monotonous chant as though she had not seen me at all.

'And the child you heard crying?' I ventured to ask.

'Oh! How can I tell what it was? I don't know,' she answered with impatient perplexity. 'I can't believe that it was the spirit of little Dot, and yet—and yet—what was it?'

From *East of Suez* (1926)

THURNLEY ABBEY

Perceval Landon

Three years ago I was on my way out to the East, and as an extra day in London was of some importance, I took the Friday evening mail-train to Brindisi instead of the usual Thursday morning Marseilles Express. Many people shrink from the long forty-eight hour train journey through Europe, and the subsequent rush across the Mediterranean on the nineteen-knot *Isis* or *Osiris;* but there is really very little discomfort on either the train or the mail-boat, and unless there is actually nothing for one to do, I always like to save the extra day and a half in London before I say goodbye to her for one of my longer tramps. This time—it was early, I remember, in the shipping season, probably about the beginning of September—there were few passengers, and I had a compartment in the P&O Indian Express to myself all the way from Calais. All Sunday I watched the blue waves dimpling the Adriatic, and the pale rosemary along the cuttings; the plain white towns, with their flat roofs and their bold 'duomos', and the grey-green gnarled olive orchards of Apulia. The journey was just like any other. We ate in the dining car as often and as long as we decently could. We slept after luncheon; we dawdled the afternoon away with yellow-backed novels; sometimes we exchanged platitudes in the smoking room, and it was there that I met Alastair Colvin.

Colvin was a man of middle height, with a resolute, well-cut jaw; his hair was turning grey; his moustache was sun-whitened, otherwise he was clean-shaven—obviously a gentleman, and obviously also a preoccupied man. He had no great wit. When spoken to, he made the usual remarks in the right way, and I dare say he refrained from banalities only because he spoke less than the rest of us; most of the time he buried himself in the Wagon-lit Company's timetable, but seemed unable to concentrate his attention on any one page of it. He found that I had been over the Siberian railway, and for a quarter of an hour he discussed it with me. Then he lost interest in it, and rose to go to his compartment. But he came back again very soon, and seemed glad to pick up the conversation again.

Of course, this did not seem to me to be of any importance. Most travellers by train become a trifle infirm of purpose after thirty-six hours' rattling. But Colvin's restless way I noticed in somewhat marked contrast with the man's personal importance and dignity; especially ill-suited was it to his finely made large hand with strong, broad, regular nails and its few lines. As I looked at his hand I noticed a long, deep, and recent scar of ragged shape. However, it is absurd to pretend that I thought anything was unusual. I went off at five o'clock on Sunday afternoon to sleep away the hour or two that had still to be got through before we arrived at Brindisi.

Once there, we few passengers transhipped our hand baggage, verified our berths—there were only a score of us in all—and then, after an aimless ramble of half an hour in Brindisi, we returned to dinner at the Hotel International, not wholly surprised that the town had been the death of Virgil. If I remember rightly, there is a gaily painted hall at the

International—I do not wish to advertize anything, but there is no other place in Brindisi at which to await the coming of the mails—and after dinner I was looking with awe at a trellis overgrown with blue vines, when Colvin moved across the room to my table. He picked up *Il Secolo,* but almost immediately gave up the pretence of reading it. He turned squarely to me and said,

'Would you do me a favour?'

One doesn't do favours to stray acquaintances on Continental Expresses without knowing something more of them than I knew of Colvin. But I smiled in a non-committal way, and asked him what he wanted. I wasn't wrong in part of my estimate of him; he said bluntly,

'Will you let me sleep in your cabin on the *Osiris?*' And he coloured a little as he said it.

Now, there is nothing more tiresome than having to put up with a stable-companion at sea, and I asked him rather pointedly, 'Surely, there is room for all of us?' I thought that perhaps he had been partnered off with some mangy Levantine, and wanted to escape from him at all hazards.

Colvin, still somewhat confused, said, 'Yes; I am in a cabin by myself. But you would do me the greatest favour if you would allow me to share yours.'

This was all very well, but, besides the fact that I always sleep better when alone, there had been some recent thefts on board English liners, and I hesitated, frank and honest and self-conscious as Colvin was. Just then the mail-train came in with a clatter and a rush of escaping steam, and I asked him to see me again about it on the boat when we started. He answered me curtly—I suppose he saw the mistrust in my manner—'I am a member of White's.' I smiled to myself as he said it, but I remembered in a moment that the man—if he were really what he claimed to be, and I make no doubt that he was—must have been sorely put to it before he urged the fact as a guarantee of his respectability to a total stranger at a Brindisi hotel.

That evening, as we cleared the red and green harbour-lights of Brindisi, Colvin explained. This is his story in his own words.

'When I was travelling in India some years ago, I made the acquaintance of a youngish man in the Forests Service. We camped out together for a week, and I found him a pleasant companion. John Broughton was a light-hearted soul when off duty, but a steady and capable man in any of the small emergencies that continually arise in that department. He was liked and trusted by Indians and though a trifle over-pleased with himself when he escaped to civilization at Simla or Calcutta, Broughton's future was well-assured in government service, when a fair-sized estate was unexpectedly left to him, and he joyfully shook the dust to the Indian plains from his feet and returned to England. For five years he drifted about London. I saw him now and then. We dined together about every eighteen months, and I could trace pretty exactly the gradual sickening of Broughton with a merely idle life. He then set out on a couple of long voyages, returned as restless as before, and at last told me that he had decided to marry and settle down at his place, Thurnley Abbey, which had long been empty. He spoke about looking after the property and standing for his constituency in the usual way. Vivien Wilde, his fiancée, had, I suppose, begun to take him in hand. She was a pretty girl with a deal of fair hair and rather an exclusive manner; deeply religious in a narrow school, she was still kindly and high-spirited, and I thought that Broughton was in luck. He was quite happy and full of information about his future.

'Among other things, I asked him about Thurnley Abbey. He confessed that he hardly knew the place. The last tenant, a man called Clarke, had lived in one wing for fifteen years and seen no one. He had been a miser and a hermit. It was the rarest thing for a light to be seen at the Abbey after dark. Only the barest necessities of life were ordered, and the tenant himself received them at the side door. His one half-caste manservant, after a month's stay in the house, had abruptly left without warning, and had returned to the Southern States. One thing Broughton complained bitterly about: Clarke had wilfully spread the rumour among the villagers that the Abbey was haunted, and had even condescended to play childish tricks with spirit lamps and salt in order to scare trespassers away at night. He had been detected in the act of this tomfoolery, but the story spread, and no one, said Broughton, would venture near the house except in broad daylight. The hauntedness of Thurnley Abbey was now, he said with a grin, part of the gospel of the countryside, but he and his young wife were going to change all that. Would I propose myself any time I liked? I, of course, said I would, and equally, of course, intended to do nothing of the sort without a definite invitation.

'The house was put in thorough repair, though not a stick of the old furniture and tapestry were removed. Floors and ceilings were relaid: the roof was made watertight again, and the dust of half-a-century was scoured out. He showed me some photographs of the place. It was called an Abbey, though as a matter of fact it had been only the infirmary of the long vanished Abbey of Closter some five miles away. The larger part of this building remained as it had been in pre-Reformation days, but a wing had been added in Jacobean times, and that part of the house had been kept in something like repair by Mr Clarke. He had in both the ground and first floors set a heavy timber door, strongly barred with iron, in the passage between the earlier and the Jacobean parts of the house, and had entirely neglected the former. So there had been a good deal of work to be done.

'Broughton, whom I saw in London two or three times about this period, made a deal of fun over the positive refusal of the workmen to remain after sundown. Even after the electric light had been put into every room, nothing would induce them to remain, though, as Broughton observed, electric light was death on ghosts. The legend of the Abbey's ghosts had gone far and wide, and the men would take no risks. They went home in batches of five and six, and even during the daylight hours there was an inordinate amount of talking between one and another, if either happened to be out of sight of his companion. On the whole, though nothing of any sort or kind had been conjured up even by their heated imaginations during their five months' work upon the Abbey, the belief in ghosts was rather strengthened than otherwise in Thurnley because of the men's confessed nervousness, and local tradition declared itself in favour of the ghost of an immured nun.'

'"Good old nun!" said Broughton.

'I asked him whether in general he believed in the possibility of ghosts, and, rather to my surprise, he said that he couldn't say he entirely disbelieved in them. A man in India had told him one morning in camp that he believed that his mother was dead in England, as her vision had come to his tent the night before. He had not been alarmed, but had said nothing, and the figure vanished again. As a matter of fact, the next possible dak-walla brought on a telegram announcing the mother's death. "There the thing was," said Broughton. But at Thurnley he was practical enough. He roundly cursed the idiotic selfishness of Clarke, whose silly antics had caused all the inconvenience. At the same time, he couldn't refuse to sympathize to some extent with the ignorant workmen. "My own idea," said he, "is that if a ghost ever does come in one's way, one ought to speak to it."

'I agreed. Little as I knew of the ghost world and its conventions, I had always remembered that a spook was in honour bound to wait to be spoken to. It didn't seem much to do, and I felt that the sound of one's own voice would at any rate reassure oneself as to one's wakefulness. But there are few ghosts outside Europe—few, that is, that a white man can see—and I had never been troubled with any. However, as I have said, I told Broughton that I agreed.

'So the wedding took place, and I went to it in a tall hat which I bought for the occasion, and the new Mrs Broughton smiled very nicely at me afterwards. As it had to happen, I took the Orient Express that evening and was not in England again for nearly six months. Just before I came back I got a letter from Broughton. He asked if I could see him in London or come to Thurnley, as he thought I should be better able to help him than anyone else he knew. His wife sent a nice message to me at the end, so I was reassured about at least one thing. I wrote from Budapest that I would come and see him at Thurnley two days after my arrival in London, and as I sauntered out of the Pannonia into the Kerepesi Utcza to post my letters, I wondered of what earthly service I could be to Broughton. I had been out with him after tiger on foot, and I could imagine few men better able at a pinch to manage their own business. However, I had nothing to do, so after dealing with some small accumulations of business during my absence, I packed a kit-bag and departed to Euston.

'I was met by Broughton's great limousine at Thurnley Road station, and after a drive of nearly seven miles we echoed through the sleepy streets of Thurnley village, into which the main gates of the park thrust themselves, splendid with pillars and spread eagles and tomcats rampant atop of them. I never was a herald, but I know that the Broughtons have the right to supporters—Heaven knows why! From the gates a quadruple avenue of beech trees led inwards for a quarter of a mile. Beneath them, a neat strip of fine turf edged the road and ran back until the poison of the dead beech leaves killed it under the trees. There were many wheel tracks on the road, and a comfortable little pony trap jogged past me laden with a country parson and his wife and daughter. Evidently there was some garden party going on at the Abbey. The road dropped away to the right at the end of the avenue, and I could see the Abbey across a wide pasturage and a broad lawn thickly dotted with guests.

'The end of the building was plain. It must have been almost mercilessly austere when it was first built, but time had crumbled the edges and toned the stone down to an orange-lichened grey wherever it showed behind its curtain of magnolia, jasmine and ivy. Farther on was the three-storeyed Jacobean house, tall and handsome. There had not been the slightest attempt to adapt the one to the other, but the kindly ivy had glossed over the touching point. There was a tall fleche in the middle of the building, surmounting a small, bell tower. Behind the house there rose the mountainous verdure of Spanish chestnuts all the way up the hill.

'Broughton had seen me coming from afar, and walked across from his other guests to welcome me before turning me over to the butler's care. This man was sandy-haired and rather inclined to be talkative. He could, however, answer hardly any questions about the house; he had, he said, only been there three weeks. Mindful of what Broughton had told me, I made no inquiries about ghosts, though the room into which I was shown might have justified anything. It was a very large low room with oak beams projecting from the white ceiling. Every inch of the walls, including the doors, was covered with tapestry, and a remarkably fine Italian four post bedstead, heavily draped, added to the darkness and dignity of the place. All the furniture was old, well-made, and dark. Underfoot there was a plain green pile carpet, the only new thing about the room except the electric light fittings and the jugs and basins. Even the looking glass on the dressing table was an old pyramidal Venetian glass, set in heavy repousse frame of tarnished silver.

'After a few minutes' cleaning up, I went downstairs and out upon the lawn, where I greeted my hostess. The people gathered there were of the usual country type, all anxious to be pleased and roundly curious as to the new master of the Abbey. Rather to my surprise, and quite to my pleasure, I rediscovered Glenham, whom I had known well in old days in Barotseland; he lived quite close, as, he remarked with a grin, I ought to have known. "But," he added, "I don't live in a place like this." He swept his hand to the long, low lines of the Abbey in obvious admiration, and then, to my intense interest, muttered beneath his breath, "Thank God!" He saw that I had overheard him, and turning to me said decidedly, "Yes, 'thank God' I said, and I meant it. I wouldn't live at the Abbey for all of Broughton's money."

"But surely," I demurred, "you know that old Clarke was discovered in the very act of setting light to his bug-a-boos?"

'Glenham shrugged his shoulders. "Yes, I know about that. But there is something wrong with the place still. All I can say is that Broughton is a different man since he has lived here. I don't believe that he will remain much longer. But—you're staying here? Well, you'll hear all about it tonight. There's a big dinner, I understand." The conversation turned off to old reminiscences, and Glenham soon after had to go.

'Before I went to dress that evening I had twenty minutes'

talk with Broughton in his library. There was no doubt that the man was altered, gravely altered. He was nervous and fidgety, and I found him looking at me only when my eye was off him. I naturally asked him what he wanted of me. I told him I would do anything I could, but that I couldn't conceive what he lacked that I could provide. He said with a lustreless smile that there was, however, something, and that he would tell me the following morning. It struck me that he was somehow ashamed of himself. And perhaps ashamed of the part he was asking me to play. However, I dismissed the subject from my mind and went up to dress in my palatial room. As I shut the door a draught blew out the Queen of Sheba from the wall, and I noticed that the tapestries were not fastened to the wall at the bottom. I have always held very practical views about spooks, and it has often seemed to me that the slow waving in firelight of loose tapestry upon a wall would account for ninety-nine per cent of the stories one hears. Certainly, the dignified undulation of this lady with her attendants and huntsmen—one of whom was untidily cutting the throat of a fallow deer upon the very steps on which King Solomon, a grey-faced Flemish nobleman with the order of the Golden Fleece awaited his fair visitor—gave colour to my hypothesis.

'Nothing much happened at dinner. The people were very much like those of the garden party. A young woman next to me seemed anxious to know what was being read in London. As she was far more familiar than I with the most recent magazines and literary supplements, I found salvation in being myself instructed in the tendencies of modern fiction. All true art, she said, was shot through and through with melancholy. How vulgar were the attempts at wit that marked so many modern books! From the beginning of literature it had always been tragedy that embodied the highest attainment of every age. To call such works morbid merely begged the question. No thoughtful man—she looked sternly at me through the steel rim of her glasses—could fail to agree with me. Of course, as one would, I immediately and properly said that I slept with Pett Ridge and Jacobs under my pillow at night, and that if *Jorrocks* weren't quite so large and cornery, I would add him to the company. She hadn't read any of them, so I was saved—for a time. But I remember grimly that she said that the clearest wish of her life was to be in some awful and soul-freezing situation of horror, and I remember that she dealt hardly with the hero of Nat Paynter's vampire story, between nibbles at her brown bread ice. She was a cheerless soul, and I couldn't help thinking that if there were many such in the neighbourhood, it was not surprising that old Glenham had been stuffed with some nonsense or the other about the Abbey. Yet, nothing could well have been less creepy than the glitter of silver and glass, and the subdued lights and cackle of conversation all round the dinner table.

'After the ladies had gone I found myself talking to the rural dean. He was a thin, earnest man, who at once turned the conversation to old Clarke's buffooneries. But, he said, Mr Broughton had introduced such a new and cheerful spirit, not only into the Abbey, but, he might say, into the whole neighbourhood, that he had great hopes that the ignorant superstitions of the past were from henceforth destined to oblivion. Thereupon his other neighbour, a portly gentleman of independent means and position, audibly remarked "Amen", which damped the rural dean, and we talked of partridges past, partridges present and pheasants to come. At the other end of the table Broughton sat with a couple of his friends, red-faced hunting men. Once I noticed that they were discussing me, but I paid no attention to it at the time. I remembered it a few hours later.

'By eleven all the guests were gone, and Broughton, his wife, and I were alone together under the fine plaster ceiling of the Jacobean drawing room. Mrs Broughton talked about one or two of the neighbours, and then, with a smile, said that she knew I would excuse her, shook hands with me, and went off to bed. I am not very good at analysing things, but I felt that she talked a little uncomfortably and with a suspicion of effort, smiled rather conventionally, and was obviously glad to go. These things seem trifling enough to repeat, but I had throughout the faint feeling that everything was not square. Under the circumstances, this was enough to set me wondering what on earth the service could be that I was to render—wondering also whether the whole business were not some ill-advised jest in order to make me come down from London for a mere shooting-party.

'Broughton said little after she had gone. But he was evidently labouring to bring the conversation round to the so-called haunting of the Abbey. As soon as I saw this, of course I asked him directly about it. He then seemed at once to lose interest in the matter. There was no doubt about it; Broughton was somehow a changed man, and to my mind he had changed in no way for the better. Mrs Broughton seemed no sufficient cause. He was clearly very fond of her, and she of him. I reminded him that he was going to tell me what I could do for him in the morning, pleaded my journey, lighted a candle, and went upstairs with him. At the end of the passage leading into the old house he grinned weakly and said, "Mind, if you see a ghost, do talk to it; you said you would." He stood irresolutely a moment and then turned away. At the door of his dressing room he paused once more. "I'm here," he called out, "if you should want anything. Good night," and he shut his door.

'I went along the passage to my room, undressed, switched on a lamp beside my bed, read a few pages of *The Jungle Book*, and then, more than ready for sleep, turned the light off and went fast asleep.

'Three hours later I woke up. There was not a breath of wind outside. There was not even a flicker of light from the fireplace. As I lay there, an ash tinkled slightly as it cooled, but there was hardly a gleam of the dullest red in the grate. An owl cried among the silent Spanish chestnuts on the slope outside. I idly reviewed the events of the day, hoping that I should fall off to sleep again before I reached dinner. But at the end I seemed as wakeful as ever. There was no help for it. I must read my *Jungle Book* again till I felt ready to go off, so I fumbled for the pear at the end of the cord that hung down inside the bed, and I switched on the bedside lamp. The sudden glory dazzled me for a moment. I felt under my pillow for my book with half-shut eyes. Then, growing used to the light, I happened to look down to the foot of my bed.

'I can never tell you really what happened then. Nothing I could ever confess in the most abject words could even faintly picture to you what I felt. I know that my heart stopped dead, and my throat shut automatically. In one instinctive movement I crouched back up against the headboards of the bed, staring at the horror. The movement set my heart going again, and the sweat dripped from every pore. I am not a particularly religious man, but I had always believed that God would never allow any supernatural appearance to present itself to man in such a guise and in such circumstances that harm, either bodily or mental, could result to him. I can only tell you that at that moment both my life and my reason rocked unsteadily on their seats.

The other *Osiris* passengers had gone to bed. Only he and I remained leaning over the starboard railing, which rattled uneasily now and then under the fierce vibration of the over-engined mail-boat. Far over, there were the lights of a few fishing-smacks riding out the night, and a great rush of white combing and seething water fell out and away from us overside.

At last Colvin went on:

'Leaning over the foot of my bed, looking at me, was a figure swathed in a rotten and tattered veiling. This shroud passed over the head, but left both eyes and the right side of the face bare. It then followed the line of the arm down to where the hand grasped the bed-end. The face was not entirely that of a skull, though the eyes and the flesh of the face were totally gone. There was a thin, dry skin drawn tightly over the features, and there was some skin left on the hand. One wisp of hair crossed the forehead. It was perfectly still. I looked at it, and it looked at me, and my brains turned dry and hot in my head. I had still got the pear of the electric lamp in my hand, and I played idly with it; only I dared not turn the light out again. I shut my eyes, only to open them in a hideous terror the same second. The thing had not moved My heart was thumping, and the sweat cooled me as it evaporated. Another cinder tinkled in the grate, and a panel creaked in the wall.

'My reason failed me. For twenty minutes, or twenty seconds, I was able to think of nothing else but this awful figure, till there came, hurtling through the empty channels of my senses, the remembrance that Broughton and his friends had discussed me furtively at dinner. The dim possibility of its being a hoax stole gratefully into my unhappy mind, and once there, one's pluck came creeping back along a thousand tiny veins. My first sensation was one of blind unreasoning thankfulness that my brain was going to stand the trial. I am not a timid man, but the best of us needs some human handle to steady him in time to extremity, and in this faint but growing hope that after all it might be only a brutal hoax, I found the fulcrum that I needed. At last I moved.

'How I managed to do it I cannot tell you, but with one spring towards the foot of the bed I got within arm's length and struck out one fearful blow with my fist at the thing. It crumbled under it, and my hand was cut to the bone. With a sickening revulsion after my terror, I dropped half-fainting across the end of the bed. So it was merely a foul trick after all. No doubt the trick had been played many a time before; no doubt Broughton and his friends had had some large bet among themselves as to what I should do when I discovered the gruesome thing. From my state of abject terror I found myself transported into an insensate anger. I shouted curses upon Broughton. I dived rather than climbed over the bed- end on to the sofa. I tore at the robed skeleton—how well the whole thing had been carried out, I thought—I broke the skull against the floor, and stamped upon its dry bones. I flung the head away under the bed, and rent the brittle bones of the trunk in pieces. I snapped the thin thigh bones across my knee, and flung them in different directions. The shin-bones I set up against a stool and broke with my heel. I raged like a Berserker against the loathly thing, and stripped the ribs from the backbone and slung the breastbone against the cupboard. My fury increased as the work of destruction went on. I tore the frail rotten veil into twenty pieces, and the dust went up over everything, over the clean blotting paper and the silver inkstand. At last my work was done. There was but a raffle of broken bones and strips of parchment and crumbling wool. Then, picking up a piece of the skull—it was the cheek and temple bone of the right side, I remember—I opened the door and went down the passage to Broughton's dressing room. I remember still how my sweat dripping pyjamas clung to me as I walked. At the door I kicked and entered.

'Broughton was in bed. He had already turned the light on and seemed shrunken and horrified. For a moment he could hardly pull himself together. Then I spoke. I don't know what I said. Only I know that from a heart full and overfull with hatred and contempt, spurred on by shame of my own recent cowardice, I let my tongue run on. He answered nothing. I was amazed at my own fluency. My hair still clung lankily to my wet temples, my hand was bleeding profusely, and I must have looked a strange sight. Broughton huddled himself up at the head of the bed just as I had. Still he made no answer, no answer, no defence. He seemed preoccupied with something besides my reproaches, and once or twice moistened his lips with his tongue. But he could say nothing though he moved his hands now and then, just as a baby who cannot speak moves its hands.

'At last the door into Mrs Broughton's room opened and she came in, white and terrified. "What is it? What is it? Oh, in God's name! What is it?" she cried again and again, and then she went up to her husband and sat on the bed in her nightdress, and the two faced me. I told her what the matter was. I spared her husband not a word for her presence there. Yet, he seemed hardly to understand. I told the pair that I had spoiled their cowardly joke for them. Broughton looked up.

'"I have smashed the foul thing into a hundred pieces," I said. Broughton licked his lips again and his mouth worked. "By God!" I shouted, "it would serve you right if I thrashed you within an inch of your life. I will take care that not a decent man or woman of my acquaintance ever speaks to you again. And there," I added, throwing the broken piece of the skull upon the floor beside his bed, "there is a souvenir for you, of your damned work tonight!"

'Broughton saw the bone, and in a moment it was his turn

to frighten me. He squealed like a hare caught in a trap. He screamed and screamed till Mrs Broughton, almost as bewildered as myself, held on to him and coaxed him like a child to be quiet. But Broughton—and as he moved I thought that ten minutes ago I perhaps looked as terribly ill as he did—thrust her from him, and scrambled out of the bed on to the floor, and still screaming put out his hand to the bone. It had blood on it from my hand. He paid no attention to me whatever. In truth I said nothing. This was a new turn indeed to the horrors of the evening. He rose from the floor with the bone in his hand and stood silent. He seemed to be listening. "Time, time, perhaps," he muttered, and almost at the same moment fell at full length on the carpet, cutting his head against the fender. The bone flew from his hand and came to rest near the door. I picked Broughton up, haggard and broken, with blood over his face. He whispered hoarsely and quickly, "Listen, listen!" We listened.

'After ten seconds' utter quiet, I seemed to hear something. I could not be sure, but at last there was no doubt. There was a quiet sound as of one moving along the passage. Little regular steps came towards us over the hard oak flooring. Broughton moved to where his wife sat, white and speechless, on the bed, and pressed her face into his shoulder.

'Then, the last thing that I could see as he turned the light out, he fell forward with his own head pressed into the pillow of the bed. Something in their company, something in their cowardice, helped me, and I faced the open doorway of the room, which was outlined fairly clearly against the dimly lighted passage. I put out one hand and touched Mrs Broughton's shoulder in the darkness. But at the last moment I too failed. I sank on my knees and put my face in the bed. Only we all heard. The footsteps came to the door, and there they stopped.

The piece of bone was lying a yard inside the door. There was a rustle of moving stuff, and the thing was in the room. Mrs Broughton was silent. I could hear Broughton's voice praying, muffled in the pillow; I was cursing my own cowardice. Then the steps moved out again on the oak boards of the passage, and I heard the sounds dying away. In a flash of remorse I went to the door and looked out. At the end of the corridor I thought I saw something that moved away. A moment later the passage was empty. I stood with my forehead against the jamb of the door almost physically sick.

'"You can turn the light on," I said, and there was an answering flare. There was no bone at my feet. Mrs Broughton had fainted. Broughton was almost useless, and it took me ten minutes to bring her to. Broughton only said one thing worth remembering. For the most part he went on muttering prayers. But I was glad afterwards to recollect that he had said that thing. He said in a colourless voice, half as a question, half as a reproach, "You didn't speak to her."

'We spent the remainder of the night together. Mrs Broughton actually fell off into a kind of sleep before dawn, but she suffered so horribly in her dreams that I shook her into consciousness again. Never was dawn so long in coming. Three or four times Broughton spoke to himself. Mrs Broughton would then just tighten her hold on his arm, but she could say nothing. As for me, I can honestly say that I grew worse as the hours passed and the light strengthened. The two violent reactions had battered down my steadiness of view, and I felt that the foundations of my life had been built upon the sand. I said nothing, and after binding up my hand with a towel, I did not move. It was better so. They helped me and I helped them, and we all three knew that our reason had gone very near to ruin that night. At last, when the light came in pretty strongly, and the birds outside were chattering and singing, we felt that we must do something. Yet we never moved. You might have thought that we should particularly dislike being found as we were by the servants; yet nothing of that kind mattered a straw, and an overpowering listlessness bound us as we sat, until Chapman, Broughton's man, actually knocked and opened the door. None of us moved. Broughton, speaking hardly and stiffly, said, "Chapman, you can come back in five minutes." Chapman, was a discreet man, but it would have made no difference to us if he had carried his news to the "room" at once.

'We looked at each other and I said I must go back. I meant to wait outside till Chapman returned. I simply dared not re-enter my bedroom alone. Broughton roused himself and said that he would come with me. Mrs Broughton agreed to remain in her own room for five minutes if the blinds were drawn up and all the doors left open.

'So Broughton and I, leaning stiffly one against the other, went down to my room. By the morning light that filtered past the blinds we could see our way, and I released the blinds. There was nothing wrong in the room from end to end, except smears of my own blood at the end of the bed, on the sofa, and on the carpet where I had torn the thing to pieces.'

Colvin had finished his story. There was nothing to say. Seven bells stuttered out from the fo'c'sle, and the answering cry wailed through the darkness. I took him downstairs.

'Of course, I am much better now, but it is a kindness of you to let me sleep in your cabin.'

GONE FISHING

Ruskin Bond

The house was called 'Undercliff', because that's where it stood—under a cliff. The man who went away—the owner of the house was Robert Astley. And the man who stayed behind—the old family retainer—was Prem Bahadur.

Astley had been gone many years. He was still a bachelor in his late thirties when he'd suddenly decided that he wanted adventure, romance, faraway places; and he'd given the keys of the house to Prem Bahadur—who'd served the family for thirty years—and had set off on his travels.

Someone saw him in Sri Lanka. He'd been heard of in Burma, around the ruby mines at Mogok. Then he turned up in Java, seeking a passage through the Sunda Straits. After that the trail petered out. Years passed. The house in the hill station remained empty.

But Prem Bahadur was still there, living in an outhouse.

Every day he opened up Undercliff, dusted the furniture in all the rooms, made sure that the bedsheets and pillowcases were clean, and set out Astley's dressing gown and slippers. In the old days, whenever Astley had come home after a journey or a long tramp in the hills, he had liked to bathe and change into his gown and slippers, no matter what the hour. Prem Bahadur still kept them ready. He was convinced that Robert would return one day.

Astley himself had said so.

'Keep everything ready for me, Prem, old chap. I may be back after a year, or two years, or even longer, but I'll be back, I promise you. On the first of every month I want you to go to my lawyer, Mr Kapoor. He'll give you your salary and any money that's needed for the rates and repairs. I want you to keep the house tip-top?'

'Will you bring back a wife, Sahib?'

'Lord, no! Whatever put that idea in your head?'

'I thought, perhaps—because you wanted the house kept ready...'

'Ready for me, Prem. I don't want to come home and find the old place falling down.'

And so Prem had taken care of the house—although there was no news from Astley. What had happened to him? The mystery provided a talking point whenever local people met on the Mall. And in the bazaar the shopkeepers missed Astley because he was a man who spent freely.

His relatives still believed him to be alive. Only a few months back a brother had turned up—a brother who had a farm—in Canada and could not stay in India for long. He had deposited a further sum with the lawyer and told Prem to carry on as before. The salary provided Prem with his few needs. Moreover, he was convinced that Robert would return.

Another man might have neglected the house and grounds, but not Prem Bahadur. He had a genuine regard for the absent owner. Prem was much older—now almost sixty and none too strong, suffering from pleurisy and other chest troubles—but he remembered Robert as both a boy and a young man. They had been together on numerous hunting and fishing trips in the mountains. They had slept out under the stars, bathed in icy mountain streams, and eaten from the same cooking pot. Once, when crossing a small river, they had been swept downstream by a flash flood, a wall of water that came thundering down the gorges without any warning during the rainy season. Together they had struggled back to safety. Back in the hill station, Astley told everyone that Prem had saved his life; while Prem was equally insistent that he owed his life to Robert.

This year the monsoon had begun early and ended late. It dragged on through most of September, and Prem Bahadur's cough grew worse and his breathing more difficult.

He lay on his charpai on the veranda, staring out at the garden, which was beginning to get out of hand, a tangle of dahlias, snake-lilies and convolvulus. The sun finally came out. The wind shifted from the southwest to the northwest, and swept the clouds away.

Prem Bahadur had taken his charpai into the garden, and was lying in the sun, puffing at his small hookah, when he saw Robert Astley at the gate.

He tried to get up but his legs would not oblige him. The hookah slipped from his hand.

Astley came walking down the garden path and stopped in front of the old retainer, smiling down at him. He did not look a day older than when Prem Bahadur had last seen him.

'So you have come at last,' said Prem.
'I told you I'd return.'
'It has been many years. But you have not changed.'
'Nor have you, old chap.'
'I have grown old and sick and feeble.'
'You'll be fine now. That's why I've come.'
'I'll open the house,' said Prem, and this time he found

himself getting up quite easily.

'It isn't necessary,' said Astley.

'But all is ready for you.'

'I know. I have heard of how well you have looked after everything. Come then, let's take a last look round. We cannot stay, you know.'

Prem was a little mystified but he opened the front door and took Robert through the drawing rooms and up the stairs to the bedroom. Robert saw the dressing gown and the slippers, and he placed his hand gently on the old man's shoulder.

When they returned downstairs and emerged into the sunlight, Prem was surprised to see himself—or rather his skinny body—stretched out on the charpai. The hookah lay on the ground, where it had fallen.

Prem looked at Astley in bewilderment.

'But who is that—lying there?'

'It was you. Only the husk now, the empty shell. This is the real you, standing here beside me.'

'You came for me?'

'I couldn't come until you were ready. As for me, I left my shell a long time ago. But you were determined to hang on, keeping this house together. Are you ready now?'

'And the house?'

'Others will live in it. Nothing is lost for ever, everything begins again. But come, it's time to go fishing...'

Astley took Prem by the arm, and they walked through the dappled sunlight under the deodars and finally left that place for another.